the
REDWOOD MASSACRE

A novel by Christopher Dunn

Based on the Motion Picture from Clear Focus Movies

Written & directed by David Ryan Keith

Produced by Lorraine Keith, Andrew Nicholson, Blu de Golyer & David Ryan Keith

Screenplay by David Ryan Keith & Lorraine Keith

An Elmshore Book

An Elmshore Book

Published in 2020

Copyright © 2020 Clear Focus Movies

This book is sold subject to the condition that it shall not, by way of trade or otherwise, be lent, re-sold, hired out or otherwise circulated without the copyright owners' prior consent in any form of binding or cover or other than that in which it is published and without a similar condition including this condition being imposed upon the subsequent purchaser.

This is a work of fiction. Names, places, events and incidents are either products of the writer's imagination or used fictitiously. Any resemblance to actual persons, living or dead, or actual events is purely coincidental.

Also available as an ebook

bodach

/ˈbəʊdɑːx/

noun

Scottish • Irish

noun: **bodach**; plural noun: **bodachs**

1. 1.

    a man, especially a peasant or an old man.

2. 2.

    a ghost; a spectre.

PROLOGUE

The smell was unbearable but the pain more-so. Hope was fading and she was already resigning herself to the fact the help wasn't coming. Outside the rain had stopped falling but the dripping sounds from the leaking corrugated roof had become her only comfort – hypnotic in a strange way.

How long she had been held captive she could only imagine. Covered in blood and with pain shooting through her entire body she had started to fade in and out of consciousness only to be jolted awake, if only for a few moments, from the fear and thoughts running through her mind. She doesn't know when or if he will be coming back or what his intentions are but her imagination was wandering down darkened paths with no hope seemingly in sight.

She couldn't work out where she was and her movement is extremely poor, not even enough room to stretch out her legs. She had been forced into a small, confined area – a box of sorts which was cold, damp and with a pungent smell of mold and other decaying matter. Visibility was non-existent as there was no light at all, not even the smallest of glimpses.

Faint hopes of finding a way out of her situation come in fleeting waves. She knew her family where out there so surely, it's only a matter of time until they came looking? After all, she had been in regular contact with her father ever since leaving home just under a week ago and had been updating her Instagram account on a daily basis, posting pictures and updates of the places she had visited and the foods she had eaten. The usual stuff.

With panic flowing through her head she tried hard to break free of the bindings holding both her wrists together but she was too weak and disorientated to do so. Even the dirty, blood covered gag covering her mouth was too tight to spit out.

And then there is the pain. She couldn't remember exactly what happened but the pain to the right side of her stomach and the amount of blood that had now since covered her clothes suggested something more serious was wrong. Even though she couldn't see the extent of her wounds or the blood on her clothes, she knew it was bad.

Flinching moments came and went. She knew time was now against her and she must somehow find a way to escape. But how?

The pain was too much and her breathing was starting to become erratic as she sat there, slumped up against the cold interior of the box. Closing her eyes all she could do was hope that someone would come to her rescue – but deep down she knew she couldn't hold on for much longer.

1

Wednesday, July 5th, 1972

01.20am

For the fourth night in a row he was woken from his sleep by a horrific nightmare that had the same recurring theme. The first couple of nights he put this down to working late hours and the stress of mounting debts that had started to spiral due to the farm not bringing in enough money. Footfall at the cattle auction had fallen dramatically and from the sales he did make it wasn't enough to cover both the bills and to bring in new livestock.

Outside the wind and rain buffeted the bedroom window and with the overhanging branches of trees that had grown directly outside occasionally swaying onto the building creating a loud sporadic scratching sound.

Next to him his wife slept. Nothing could wake her, not even if a hurricane was raging outside. But that was fine, she worked just as hard as he does and she needs the sleep just as much. No point in both being kept awake, night after night all because of some stupid bad dream.

Sliding his legs from under the bed covers he quietly placed his feet on the cold floor boards. Slowly making his way to the window, each footstep made a slight creaking sound but not loud enough to wake anyone, especially his wife who still fast asleep. As he peered through the window, he watched as the rain drops streaked to the bottom of the glass and build up into a pool on the sill. Now and again, branches from the trees swung forwards, scratching the outside and occasionally making him flinch backwards.

Peering out into the blackness of the night, he was still trying to process the nightmare that had awoken him. 'Why am I having these dreams' he asked himself. 'Why now?'

But tonight, it was different. Tonight, he could swear he heard someone whispering to him, like someone was in the room with him but what he heard he couldn't make out. It was just a whisper of sorts, a kind of silent noise.

Shaking his head, he tried to rationalise the scenario he was in. It was early morning, 1.20am to be precise – he knew that from glancing at the old clock that was placed on top of the dressing table at the opposite end of his bed – so apart from his wife who was still sound asleep and his two children who were in their own bedroom, he knew he was very much alone.

Suddenly, he heard a child's laugh coming from outside his bedroom. It was a faint laugh but he clearly heard it.

Making his way into the hallway he quietly closed the bedroom door behind him and made his way to his children's room where they were both sleeping. Slowly opening the door just wide enough to peer into the room he stared into the darkness for a few seconds to try and see any signs of activity.

"Morgan" he quietly whispered. Pausing for a second he tried again. "Jacob, have any of you been out of your room tonight?"

Nothing. He waited a for a few moments and then stood back into the hallway, closing the door behind him. Neither of the them had been playing around so he must be imagining the laughter it seemed.

The kitchen was freezing, especially the old stone floor that he was insistent in keeping when he was doing some renovation work two years ago. His wife wanted to replace the floor with something a little warmer, perhaps wooden flooring of sorts but he was having none of it and the stone remained. How he now wished he took her advice!

Taking a glass from the draining board, he turned the tap on to pour some water. He was thirsty and a glass of water, although he was already cold, seemed a good idea.

Letting the water drain for a brief moment his entire body stiffened like he had been hit with a strong electric current. Goosepimples appeared on his arms and a cold shudder ran up his back.

"Bury them." came a whisper. "Bury them all."

Thinking someone was in the kitchen with him, he quickly spun around – more in fear rather than anticipation at the sight of what he may encounter – and yet there he was, alone.

With the tap still running he slowly made his way around the large kitchen table and into the main room. The rain outside had now eased off and the only sound he could now hear was the deep breathing he was making and the water coming from the tap. Every now and then the wind buffeted the farmhouse which made a strange low tone growling sound.

Inside the main room, he stopped and looked around for any signs of an intruder but everything was silent and just as he and his wife had left things before they went to bed.

"Jesus! Man-up" he murmured to himself whilst rubbing the back of his neck.

He hadn't noticed the dark presence that had quietly crept up behind him when suddenly, after turning to go back into the kitchen, it menacingly lurched forwards forcing him to take a step back and making him fall over, knocking over a small table in the process. A glass vase with flowers that he had recently brought home as a present for his wife toppled over, smashing onto the tiled floor.

Dazed he looked up to see a faceless figure kneeling over him and with a huge pressure now resting on his chest. Hardly being able to breathe and struggling to find enough strength to push whatever this thing was off him; he could do nothing but lay there.

Looking into the seemingly black space where a face should be, his head started to fill with horrible visions. Bodies, blood-soaked bodies lying in a field – seemingly butchered with body parts left strewn around on the ground. Not just one or two bodies, but hundreds of bodies covering acres of fields that he had no recollection of and everywhere and everything including the sky, the grass, the pathways – everything seemed to be in a dull shade of red. No greens, blues or yellows – just a dull red. There was also a god-awful smell that transcended into the air, something of which he had never encountered before but it was also attracting large plumes of flies that were feasting eagerly on the rotting corpses. Then there were the crows. Hundreds, if not thousands of crows blanketing the deep red sky, circling and then plummeting to the ground to join in with the feast that the flies had already started on.

And just as quickly as the presence had forced him to the floor and the visions had begun, darkness replaced the bloody images that had been impregnated into his mind. Slowly drifting into and out of consciousness, he lay on the floor – wet from the broken vase he had knocked over and yet he still couldn't muster the strength to move. Closing his eyes, he could do nothing other than prey that these hallucinations would not come back.

2

Present Day

Pulling up outside Kirsty's parents' house, Mark honked on the horn of his newly purchased four-by-four. After months of working long hours and putting every penny earned into a savings account, he had finally been able to get his hands on a brand-new car. His obsession with it had caused a few arguments between him and Kirsty over the last few months but he managed to pacify her by promising her a fantastic holiday in the near future to a destination of her choice.

It took a couple of minutes before Kirsty appeared at the door, struggling to carry a rather large looking suitcase.

"Well you could at least give me a hand!" she shouted over to Mark as he was getting out of the car.

"Quick question Kirsty; where do you think we are going this weekend? I told you to keep things small and simple!" he quipped.

"If you think I'm going to wear the same clothes over the next couple of days then you'd better think again, Mark."

"Two days Kirsty – that's all. I think you have packed for a week's trip from the look of things!" he replied.

Picking up the suitcase he walked back to his car and placed it into the boot. "See here, this is all you need." pointing to his backpack.

Unamused, Kirsty looked at Mark and was quick to remind him that it was his idea to go camping in the first place. "Well, if you don't like it, I can always stay here whilst you go off playing campers with your friends." she replied.

Knowing he would never win an argument with Kirsty; he closed the boot of the car and made his way around to the driver's side.

"OK, you win. No point wasting time arguing. Let's get on the road and just enjoy the weekend yeah?"

"Err, Mark – whatever happened to the gentleman opening the door for the lady?" she teasingly asked.

"Just get in the car Kirsty" Mark replied.

"OK, OK - it's only a joke Mark, only a joke!"

"And don't – "

The door slammed shut as Kirsty made herself comfortable in the passenger seat. Reaching over her shoulder to grab hold of the seat-belt she was about to fasten it when she noticed Mark staring at her.

"Slam the door" he continued.

Surrounded by the stunning views of the Scottish Highlands that contained hidden glens and spectacular cliffs, the long winding roads seemingly led from one small village to another – unchanged by modern advancements in twenty-first housing developments. Small stone-built houses and quaint little Inns that were built some three-hundred years ago had survived the variant Scottish climate and no amount of blistering cold winds, rain and storms could touch their beauty – these were built to last!

The scenery also matched the many myths and legends from Scottish folklore with tales of epic clan battles to mythical fairies and monsters that still roam the wilderness. It was as beautiful as it was menacing.

"It's stunning out here." Kirsty, with her head leaning on the window, softly spoke.

"Yeah it is. It's like time has stood still in some of these parts." Mark replied. "Maybe we should plan to stay over at one of these places sometime?"

Turning her head to face him, Kirsty may well have liked the scenery but she wasn't hinting at spending any more time in the middle of nowhere.

"I don't think so. It's nice and all but what is there to do out here? Oh wait, I know, let's go hiking!" she sarcastically remarked.

"It'll do you good to get out of the city once in a while Kirsty – you know, to breathe in the fresh air, get real air into your lungs. And out here you wouldn't be distracted by your phone every five minutes."

"Well I'll give you that!" she replied. "There is no chance I'll get a signal out here."

Laughing, Mark for the first time during the journey was feeling a little more relaxed as Kirsty had been complaining throughout the week about spending time out in the woods camping. It also didn't help that she would be spending time with people she didn't know or didn't like.

"I just hope where we are going is just as nice – it will ease the pain of being around Jessica I guess." Kirsty spoke with a tinge of annoyance.

"What winds me up about her is that she is always right; always trying to get the better of me no matter what I say or do."

"You just need to bite you tongue Kirsty. Just don't let her get to you." Mark replied.

"I know what she can be like and yes she does like to be the center of attention most of the time but you – "

"Most of the time? You kidding me – its ALL of the time!" Kirsty quickly corrected Mark.

"Look, just don't rise to her. Walk away, ignore her – just don't rise to her OK."

Mark knew what he was saying wouldn't make any difference – both Kirsty and Jessica had the same mentality and neither would back down from any arguments they may have during the course of the weekend.

3

Sat on a wall opposite the magnificent Greyfriars Church, Pamela cursed as she rummaged around in her backpack. She had put the earphones for her mobile phone inside when packing but they had somehow managed to worm their way in between the various items and clothing she had convinced herself she would be needing over the course of the next two days.

"You got to be kidding me!" she muttered, finally spotting the white cord that had somehow wrapped itself around the plastic bristles of her hairbrush. "How? How the hell does that happen!"

After a few minutes of fiddling with the tangled mess and repacking some of the items she had to remove just to free the earphones, Pamela flicked through the collection of music she had stored on her phone before hitting the play button.

Humming to Madonna's – 'Like a Prayer', Pamela sat and watched as people went about their daily chores.

Smirking, she saw the funny side of her song choice. "Well I guess it's appropriate!" she thought to herself as she looked up at the light grey stone that covered the church and its surroundings since its restoration. In the distance she could see workmen, in their brightly covered hi-vis jackets pointing to this, that and everything except for the pile of rubble they were all congregated around - and to her right, a bunch of school kids had made their way over the bus stop a few feet away and the old couple that had been standing there for some considerable time seemed a little put off by their appearance as they looked at each other with a look of annoyance on their faces.

It may have only been just after 8.00am in the morning but the City was slowly coming alive as cars, taxis and motorbikes endlessely passed her by. Every now and then the sound of irate drivers beeping on their car horns would echo around and she would see the odd pedestrian gesturing with their hands and arms back at the driver in question which in turn would make the driver beep on the horn even more. It just became an endless cycle until the pedestrian disappeared out view!

The City center was not one of her favorite places to visit, not ever since she was seven years old and she strayed away from her parents who frantically searched for her as she wandered around one of the many market stalls that once occupied Back Wynd.

Pamela had few recollections of that day but her parents had reminded her so many times throughout the years – enough so that she always felt anxious when visiting busy places. At heart she was a quiet person, never liking large crowds – instead preferring the solitude of what the countryside could offer her. And yet here she was, sat waiting on her own in the heart of Aberdeen City center – why did she even agree to this she began to wonder!

The school kids where making a nuisance of themselves, pushing and shoving each other in a playful but also rowdy manner making the old couple seem even more uneasy.

"Hey. Lads. Calm down will you." came a voice from the back of a crowd of people that had now entered the line.

Giggling, the two lads pushing each other paused for a moment to seemingly whisper something. Whatever was said, it made the tallest of the two laugh out loud which prompted his friend to push him again. This time however, they both moved away from the rest of their group and slumped backwards, leaning onto the wall. Well, for now at least, they had calmed down a little.

It took a further twenty-minutes or so of waiting around when suddenly Pamela felt a slight push on her shoulder. Bolting forwards and off the wall, she immediately spun around to see who had been touching her.

"Jesus Christ Jessica! You scared the shit out of me!" she said, her voice slightly shaky but grateful it was only Jessica, her best friend of all people!

"Well I did try shouting at you further back but you seemed to be in a world of your own, which isn't new!" replied Jessica.

Holding out a freshly made bacon sandwich and a hot coffee purchased from one of the many hidden cafes, Jessica wasn't going anywhere without her daily intake of caffeine.

"Here, I got you these. Thought it would help considering the day we are going to have. I still can't believe I agreed to coming on this trip this weekend."

"Aw thanks Jessica. That's so sweet."

"Ah, no worries. I kind of guessed you would be here first so I popped into the café around the corner. I don't know about you but there is no way I'm leaving on an empty stomach."

"And did you remember the brown sauce?"

"As always - not that I understand what you like about it anyway but each to their own I guess." laughed Jessica.

"Well, it's thoughtful of you anyway. How much do I owe you?"

"Jesus Pamela, I'm not going to go broke for a couple of pounds." laughed Jessica. "So, what's the plan?"

"Well, I'm finishing off this coffee and sandwich before getting the taxi to our drop off point – and I'm paying for that, no arguments!" Pamela replied.

"How long will it take to get there?"

"I think it's only around half-an-hour or so, not too long put it that way. Don't worry Jessica, I won't be bore you to death talking about Bruce if you promise not to talk about Mark – deal?"

"Ah I'd forgotten about Bruce. How is he anyway? I haven't seen him in weeks. You two still speaking to each other?" replied Jessica.

"Hey, I promised not to speak about him as long as you don't talk about Mark."

Jessica rolled her eyes at Pamela, acknowledging there will be plenty of time on this trip to talk about Bruce and Mark. "Aye, OK then." she replied.

"But you have been talking to him I presume" laughed Jessica whilst teasingly nudging Pamela to one side.

Pamela laughed, trying hard not to spill her coffee. "Hey, watch it will you."

4

The taxi was late, as always seems the case, but the driver was honest enough to admit he stopped off on the way to pick up a coffee from Costa and whilst it was only around the corner from where Pamela and Jessica where waiting, the early morning rush hour and people queuing for their own morning rituals had meant he was delayed.

"Pamela?" asked the Asian driver as he rolled down the windows on his blue Ford Mondeo.

Jessica giggled as she gave Pamela a nudge with a 'You ordered it; you can sort it' kind of attitude.

"Er, yes that's me. We are going over to Dunnottar Woods if that's possible?" she quizzingly asked the driver.

"Ah Yes, yes that's fine. And do forgive my lateness but I need my morning fix."

"Fix?"

"Oh sorry, my coffee. I needed my morning coffee you see." as he held up his now half-empty coffee cup. "Please, get in and we will be on our way." he replied

Being the closest to the rear of the taxi, Jessica opened the door to a waft of strong coffee that escaped into the morning fresh air. Making herself comfortable, Pamela tutted and started to shuffle her way around to the other side. "Help yourself Jessica why don't you." she said with a sarcastic tone in her voice.

"Hey, you had it covered!" replied Jessica.

"Right ladies, Dunnottar Woods was it. It'll take around 30 minutes to get there. Make yourselves comfortable and relax, OK?" the driver spoke in a slightly broken Scottish accent.

"Oh, don't worry. Jessica has already seen to that." mocked Pamela.

Jessica gave Pamela a poke to her ribs making her laugh in the process. "Hey, stop that!" Pamela scolded Jessica.

"My name is Raj and I'll get you there nice, safe and sound OK. Just sit back and enjoy the ride."

"Nice to meet you Raj. I'm Pamela and this is my friend Jessica."

"Nice to meet your acquaintance too." he replied.

Pulling away from their pick-up point, Raj didn't take long to start up a conversation with the girls as he quizzingly asked them about their day.

"So you girls go camping?" he asked.

"Yeah. Me and Jessica are meeting a few friends a little later and spending a couple of days over at Dunnottar." replied Pamela.

Pausing for a brief second, Raj acceptingly nodded his head before continuing with the conversation.

"Dunnottar Woods. You do know the story about what went on up there don't you?" he asked whilst staring at the girls from the mirror in his car.

"Not wanting to scare you girls but you do know the story, yeah?"

"Oh, you mean the killer farmer?" asked Jessica. "Yeah, we know of it but that was years ago so there is nothing to be afraid of now is there."

Pamela looked at Jessica and giggled as she pulled a funny face, making a strange spooky sound in the process.

"Aye your probably right but it's not a place I'd want to spend the night in." Raj replied. "No – definitely not a place for me!"

5

Leaving the relative safety of the villages behind them, Mark pulled off the main road and started to ascend along the uneven surface of a make-shift road that had been used over the years by travellers wanting to get away from the tourist hotspots. The ground was soft in places making driving a little difficult for Mark and at times he had to snatch on the steering wheel to keep the car from veering off track and onto the muddy fields.

"Bloody hell Mark! Be careful will you!" Kirsty barked.

"Last thing we want is to get stuck in these fields."

"Yeah, yeah stop worrying Kirsty. I'm not doing it on purpose!"

"We're not in a rush so just take it easy, yeah!" she replied.

"Do you want to drive? I can pull over and we can swap places if you think you can do any better?"

Mark was already stressed due to the driving conditions and Kirsty was only making matters worse.

"You would let me drive your pride and joy? OK, pull over then!" Kirsty replied in a mocking tone.

With a smirk on his face, Mark took a second to glance over at Kirsty who was fully focused on the view in front of her.

"Not a chance Kirsty" he said.

6

The first to arrive and having been travelling for a couple of hours, Kirsty had again started to pour cold water on the idea of a camping weekend. As Mark was fully aware, she wasn't keen on coming in the first place so this kind of break wasn't exactly what she would class as enjoyable – spending time hidden away in the forest. She liked her luxuries from clean and tidy five-star hotels to lazing around a pool and not having to lift a finger.

Mark on the other hand couldn't wait and this was the perfect weekend break for him. He was the kind of guy that likes to keep things simple and being out in the forest was what he knew, after all he spent a lot of his childhood in them with his father camping and his friends making tree houses and larking around in general.

Turning into a small car park situated on the outskirts of the woods, Mark was relieved to finally arrive.

"Well, we're here. Safe and sound at least." he said.

Looking out of the window Kirsty stared at the open space around her.

"No-one else here, I wonder why? Oh, I know why – because it's a bloody forest with nothing to do!" she unamusingly replied.

"Seriously Mark, are we really going to do this?"

"Aw come-on Kirsty, at least give it a go – who knows, maybe you might like camping?"

"Yeah right!" she replied.

Opening the door, Mark left the car, beckoning Kirsty to join him.

"No point in wasting time. It'll be dark before we know it so we better get a move on." he said.

Kirsty watched on as Mark went to the back of his car and opened the boot. Taking out his backpack first she rolled her eyes, tutted to herself and finally mustered the energy to help him.

"Aw man! Just look at the state of this!" Mark snarled, looking at the amount of mud that had been plastered over his car.

"Oh dear. Is your car all dirty Mark? What a shame." laughed Kirsty.

Unamused, Mark started to take her belongings out from the boot, putting them down on the ground next to his car.

"Hey, be careful with that, I've got expensive things in there" she shouted to Mark as her suitcase slipped from his hands. She really didn't want to be on *this* kind of holiday!

"Look, Kirsty – you do realize were not staying in a five-star hotel this weekend?" he replied whilst fumbling around picking up the suitcase.

"Remember, this was your idea not mine" she replied in curt manner. Mark looked sheepish as she continued moaning. "Spending the weekend with your ditsy ex-girlfriend isn't exactly gonna be any fun for me, is it?"

Without wanting to start the weekend off with any lingering feelings, Mark tried to calm the situation down with some reassuring words that fell on deaf ears.

"Trust me – this is going to be one weekend you will never forget – I promise".

"That's what I'm worried about." she muttered under her breath as she turned away from him.

"What was that?" asked Mark.

"Nothing Mark, it was nothing."

"Well, look after yourselves girls and have a great weekend" said Raj as he tried to give Pamela some change from the twenty-pound note she had just handed him.

"No, keep it. And thanks for getting us here safe and sound Raj." Pamela replied.

"Oh, you're too kind. Too kind but thank you." he spoke, putting the loose change into a plastic cup that he no-doubted had been using for tips.

"Right, onto my next pick-up. Stay safe girls."

Raj slowly reversed his car backwards and started to make his way back through the narrow lane he had just come from before slowly disappearing out of sight.

"Well, just me, you and the woods now Pamela." Jessica teased, tamely patting Pamela on her shoulder. "Come on – let's get moving."

7

For almost an hour, Jessica and Pamela had been making their way deep into the heart of the woods, taking in the beauty and tranquility of the scenery around them. The route they had taken had placed them further afield and away from most ramblers who frequently visited the woods and but for the odd person or two who may have strayed off the official walkways, they were all alone. The silence made them feel at ease and considering where they were going, they never at any point felt any concerns or regrets as to their choice of weekend break.

Having known each other for many years their talks had been about Mark and Kirsty and how the gang would all get on with each other when they eventually meet up. Pamela got the feeling that things would be a little awkward once Jessica and Kirsty met but she also knew Jessica well enough to know that she could easily take care of herself.

"I'm praying Kirsty has pulled out of this trip, I really am." Jessica said jokingly.

"If not, it's going to be a long weekend."

"Aw come on Jess, she's not all that bad. Yeah, she can be a little annoying I guess but she's harmless enough. Plus, you're a big girl who can look after herself!" smiled Pamela.

"Pamela, you know as well as me that she is just full of herself. It's always me, me, me with her, like no-one else matters. "

"You sure your just not mad because she's with Mark now and you're a little jealous?" asked Pamela.

Jessica smiled and then broke out into a laugh. "Really!" she said, pushing Pamela to one-side of the path.

"Well you guys were together for a couple of years so you must still have feelings for him?"

"Hey Pamela, I know you two are good friends and all that and I don't want to upset you but to me he's a dick. She's welcome to him!"

"OK, OK, I'll shut up about it." replied Pamela.

The two girls carried on following an uneven pathway that was situated opposite a slow flowing stream. The uneven surface was making it difficult to keep their balance as on more than one occasion, Jessica lost her footing close to the paths edge.

"Whoa Jessica – be careful will you!" said Pamela, reaching out to grab hold of Jessica's arm as she tripped.

"The last thing you need right now is to fall into that and be wet-through all evening."

"Yeah, well that would be slightly annoying as I haven't brought any spare clothes with me." replied Jessica.

"Tell me you're joking? Seriously Jessica, are you winding me up? At least tell me you brought some clean underwear with you?" Pamela teasingly laughed.

Jessica smiled. "Well obviously I've brought spare underwear – you never know who you are gonna meet in these secluded woods."

They both laughed, pushing each other from one side of the path to the other.

"Hey Pamela, are we close to where we should be heading or are we actually lost?"

"I kinda have an idea where we are." Pamela replied.

"Kinda? Well I hope your sense of direction is better than a shitty map" Jessica jokingly said.

"Well it's only us around here for miles so it shouldn't be too hard to find."

"Ah well, don't you worry, if it gets you laid, I'm sure we'll get there." Jessica said with the kind of reply you would only expect from her.

Stopping in her tracks, Pamela felt the need to thank Jessica for making the trip with her. After everything Jessica and Mark went through, she was just pleased to have her best friend with her.

"Hey, thanks for coming on the trip. You know, I don't think I would have the guts to do it without you and I know it's going to be weird with Mark there." she said.

"No, no – honestly, I'm glad I came. And anyway, I cannot wait to see the look on Kirsty's face when she finds out we're camping at the actual Redwood house." Jessica said with a mocking tone.

Wanting to have the last laugh, Pamela was quick to put Jessica back in her place. "And for your information, no one is going to be getting laid on this trip."

"We'll see" came a faint reply in the distance.

8

It had been a while since they had left the car behind and the rough terrain was already starting to take its toll on Kirsty. Mark was doing all the hard work, carrying both his and Kirsty's backpack and a suitcase through the dense woodland including listening to the constant bemoaning from Kirsty about the situation they were both in.

"Come on!" yelled Kirsty to the annoyance of Mark. "I'm coming!" he replied under his breath, not wanting to get into another argument.

Getting more frustrated, Kirsty let out a loud "*HELLO*" in the slightest of hope someone would hear but as Mark was quick to point out, they were completely alone.

"Yep, were in the middle of nowhere so no-ones gonna hear you." he muttered back.

Kirsty, not wanting to make things easy, replied in a sarcastic tone, "Well what's your big plan? Keep walking until we eventually die?" Mark, not wanting to get into anymore arguments kept quiet.

"I thought so." Kirsty responded and let out another loud "*HELLO.*"

Daylight was slowly dwindling and both knew they had to find their friends before darkness fell. At this point Kirsty still didn't know where she would be camping and whilst Mark knew it would lead to more confrontation, he just didn't have the energy to get involved in another row by telling her.

"I'm going to have stop a short while. My feet are bloody killing me." Kirsty said whilst perching herself down on a stone embankment.

"This is gonna be some weekend isn't it. You, me – JESSICA, all together in this god forsaken place!" she muttered to herself whilst -pulling off one of her boots.

"Seriously Mark, why here? And why with your ex-girlfriend?".

Mark at this point had been drinking juice from a flask he had prepared earlier and after giving a second thought to the questions of being in the forest for a weekend break and with his ex-girlfriend he bypassed both questions and simply responded with "It'll be fun. Just relax a little and *try* to enjoy it."

"Fun? You think this is FUN?" Kirsty mockingly replied. "Fun is sat in a nice, warm restaurant with a nice, warm meal relaxing to music and then perhaps, just perhaps taking a quiet walk along the beach. None of what we are doing is neither fun nor nice!"

"Whatever!" Mark snapped back. "Sometimes you have to do things in life that are not what your used to doing or what you think you are privileged to do."

"This is a weekend break. Not a weeks' vacation in the Bahamas for god's sake."

For Mark, this was big moment. It took a lot for him to get rattled but Kirsty had been pushing his buttons all day with her constant moaning. He had kept a lot of emotions locked away these last couple of hours but now he'd had enough.

"Here, take a drink. You need to keep hydrated. We shouldn't be too far away from the others now." he said in a firm manner.

Reluctantly Kirsty grabbed the flask and took a couple of sips of juice. She didn't say anything else. She didn't need to.

After wading through endless miles of bushes, nettles and damp, wet undergrowth, both Jessica and Pamela had to take a well-earned rest break. Perching herself down on a fallen tree, Pamela took her phone out to see if any messages from the rest of the group had come through, - none had. It wasn't like them but then again, it's a long trek into the woods and unless any of them were in trouble then why should they stop to send text messages?

"Bet that idiot got them lost following his own map" Jessica commented.

"Yeah, they should have been here by now." replied Pamela.

Even though it was obvious she already had, Jessica tried to comfort Pamela by asking if any of the gang had been in touch. "Have you tried calling Mark?" she asked.

"He's not answering" came a frustrared reply.

Not one for taking things seriously, Jessica then made light of things by reminding Pamela of Bruce, another friend of the pair who was due to meet up with them.

"And what about lover-boy" she taunted.

"Will you stop it Jessica, I don't know if I like him anyway" Pamela replied in a non-apologetic way.

"Yeah right. I've seen the way you look at him. It's painfully obvious to be honest."

Pamela at this point was trying her best not to blush. Yes, she did like Bruce and even she knew it was obvious to everyone but she never really talked about him in a relationship kind of way.

"Maybe I should see if he's ok?" she replied.

"Do me a favour, try and keep your drooling to a minimum." Jessica replied with a smirk on her face.

Like the others, Bruce had been on the road for quite some time, peddling through the woodland for a few hours. And just like his friends, he had found himself lost on more than one occasion.

He had known Pamela for a few years, helping her get through university and then keeping in close contact ever since. They had been on several weekend breaks together before but just as friends and he kind-of knew that Pamela had some feelings towards him but he never acted on them, instead just being a good friend and a shoulder to cry on when needed.

Having spent the last thirty minutes or so seemingly travelling in the wrong direction he stopped to take a break, checking out the map Mark had sent to him before setting off. Damn it, something was wrong after all. He had taken the wrong cycle path further back and was now going eastwards when he should have been travelling west!

Turning back and retracing his steps, he finally managed to get back on track but had only been cycling for a few minutes before his mobile phone started to ring.

"Hello"

"Hey, where are you" – came a curiosity reply from Pamela.

"Tell your friend Mark his map sucks!" Bruce jokingly replied. He was happy to hear a friendly voice on the other side of the phone. "I've just spent the past half hour heading the wrong way.".

"Do you want us to come back and get you?" Pamela asked.

Bruce didn't want to be slowed down any more and would rather get to the meeting point.

"I'll just meet you guys at the camp site. Probably quicker I just keep heading the way I'm going."

Pamela though was feeling a little guilty so tried her best to help. "Are you sure, I don't want you to get lost" she asked.

"Don't worry, I'll be right behind you" he replied.

Knowing Bruce was safe and in the knowledge he wasn't too far away, Pamela ended the conversation relieved. "Ok, well we'll see you soon." putting the phone to her chest with a smile on her face.

"Well, it's official – he's on his way". Pamela responded with some excitement in her voice.

9

Some time had passed since Pamela last spoke to Bruce and she and Jessica had walked on even further on into the woods in the hope of finding the meeting point. Jessica was becoming a little worried that they would both soon be out of options and possibly end up completely lost.

"Tell you what. You wait here and keep a look out for the others, OK?" she said to Pamela. "I'll carry on ahead and see if I can spot anything and if I do, I'll come straight back."

Pamela wasn't sure about this as the woods were densely populated with trees and bracken and the remaining daylight, they did have was quickly fading due to the canopy of taller trees making it difficult for it to break through.

"Don't stray too far away. Perhaps walk for ten minutes and no more" she begged Jessica. "But please don't wander too far off. Promise me?"

"Stop worrying Pamela! If I'm not back in ten minutes, phone lover boy for me." she replied, mocking Pamela as she wandered off and out of sight.

Pamela rolled her eyes and shook her head. She hated the term lover boy when it came to talking about Bruce but she knew Jessica was only teasing. Leaning forward looking out over a wooden constructed bridge, Pamela began thinking of the others and where they could be. She took out her mobile phone but the signal was poor. No chance of getting through to Mark or Bruce.

Putting the phone in her pocket, she looked below at the slow-moving stream beneath the bridge. *"Don't take too long Jessica."* she muttered to herself.

Kirsty and Mark where making headway and despite their differences earlier on in the day, she was still undeterred in her hatred for spending the next two days in the woods. And to make matters worse, she had been whipped and scratched by twigs and overgrown bushes and bramble, her feet were saturated from the damp ground and she was now struggling with fatigue.

"Where the hell is this place!" she snapped. "Mark, where the hell are we. Do you even know?"

"Not far now. A little further up ahead, just through that clearing and we should be there." Mark knew the end was in sight and he could not be more relieved. "Finally." he said to himself.

Looking through the tree line he saw another couple in the distance seemingly having some fun of their own. They had music playing loudly and drinking alcohol, with the lady sat in a camp chair close to a lit fire whilst the guy was stood near her, mimicking some kind of fight scene whilst frolicking around.

It looked like they weren't going to be the only ones camping in these woods this weekend.

"So, I've just found the trail!" Jessica triumphantly announced as she arrived back to the bridge where Pamela had been waiting. "It's just down past the stream."

Pamela, struggling to show any enthusiasm as it had now been a long trek shrugged her shoulders. She was becoming tired and just wanted to bed down for the evening.

"Are we really going to do this" she asked.

"Come on, you're not scared already? It's just one night." Jessica replied.

Pamela still not convinced and not wanting to put a damper on things tried her best to hide her fears, "It's not that. It's just the whole place will be full of crazy people this weekend. Why don't we just leave it for a couple of days?"

"And miss the biggest party of the year, really?" Jessica responded.

"You do know its twenty years since the murders this weekend?" replied Pamela.

Intrigued by this, Jessica couldn't wait to see for herself where the famous murders took place.

"That's the whole point. Come on, are you not just a little bit curious?"

Pausing for a second, Pamela could understand Jessica's enthusiasm.

"Well I suppose it would be nice to see what all the fuss is about."

"Exactly!" replied Jessica.

10

The meeting point had taken some time to find but most of the gang had finally made their way to it, albeit with a few cuts and grazes that could compare later when sat around the campfire. Mark and Kirsty could clearly be heard in the not too distant and it was obvious Kirsty's mood hadn't changed!

"About bloody time! Do you know how long we have been waiting for you guys?" Pamela shouted over to Mark who was struggling to keep hold of all the baggage he was carrying.

Tugging at the straps holding his back pack in place and letting it drop down to the floor, the expression on Marks face told a sorry story. He was relieved to see a much friendlier face to the one he had been travelling with for the best part of the day.

"You're lucky we are here full stop" he replied with a weary tone. "Come here and give me a hug."

Pamela didn't hesitate. She could see how much the trek had taken out of him, especially with the company he had brought with him.

Pulling away, Pamela tried to make light of the situation and ridiculed him on how much he was bringing with him.

"Are you sure you have brought enough stuff with you?" she asked.

"Ha ha, very funny" he replied. "It's so good to see you. It's been far too long."

Noticing Jessica in the distance, he flinched before looking down, trying not to make it obvious he had seen her but Pamela had already noticed.

"You OK?" she asked.

"I dunno. Are you sure this is a good idea?" he replied. Mark still had some feelings for Jessica and felt a little guilty for how they broke up. He knew it was a risk coming out to camp this weekend but he was also hopeful it would help heal a few rifts.

Turning around, Pamela saw Jessica looking down at the floor beneath her.

"She'll be fine".

"It's not her I'm worried about" replied Mark.

Meanwhile Kirsty was struggling to catch up, limping from tree to tree just to keep her balance as she had lost one of her shoes in muddy puddle a little farther back.

"For fucks sake Mark, will you help me please?" she pleaded.

Seeing Kirsty struggling to walk, a wry smile came over his face. "It's gonna be a long weekend!" to which Pamela started to laugh.

Jessica had been watching on, taking in the unravelling chaos breaking out in front of her, wondering to herself if Pamela was right when she asked if it was too soon to come out together this weekend. But she also knew it was too late to turn back now.

Making her way over to Pamela she started laughing, shaking her head in bemusement watching Mark and Kirsty making fools of themselves. Mark was trying to help Kirsty by putting her shoes back on but both of them stumbled over onto the wet floor. Mark bemoaning the fact Kirsty hadn't brought the right footwear for such a trip!

"What the hell does he see in her" Jessica asked Pamela.

Pamela didn't need to respond. She knew exactly what Jessica was getting at. Both Mark and Kirsty are like chalk and cheese, two complete opposites.

11

The couple Mark had noticed earlier on in the afternoon had by now drunk themselves into somewhat of a slumber and the alcohol had now taken its toll. Wandering off into the forest, the man was in dire need to relieve his bladder.

"I'm away for a piss alright", the words hardly coherent enough to be made out clearly.

Stumbling around in the deep undergrowth and struggling to stay on his feet, the man continued on with his drunken and yet somewhat limited vocabulary.

"You gonna go and get the rest of the beer you wee whore" he shouted.

Unzipping his trousers, the man began to urinate, splashing his feet and barely able to stand upright. Unaware as to his surroundings, he didn't see the movement just to the right of him, the overgrown leaves seemingly springing back to an upright position as if something or someone had walked through them. Whatever it was it was quick.

"Don't hear no cans opening bitch" he shouted out. Suddenly a scream could be heard in the distance. The man paused from urinating, slowly turning around facing towards where he thought the scream came from.

"What are you fucking doing?" he shouted. He waited for a few moments for a response but nothing came.

He started to urinate some more and then came another scream, this time much louder than the first. Then a noise that sounded like something hard hitting a tree followed by yet another scream.

"Daisy?" the man timidly shouted out.
Zipping his trousers up, he turned around and slowly started to make his way back towards the direction where he heard the screams coming from. "Daisy?" he kept asking.

Arriving back at his tent his partner was nowhere to be seen.

"Stop fucking about Daisy!" he said with a quiet tone in his voice. "I mean it, it's not funny!", he was now starting to get nervous and the drunken stupor he was in was quickly vanishing.

"I'm gonna kick your fucking arse for this" he said, apprehensively taking small backward steps.

Suddenly he tumbled, tripping over fallen branches around him and with nothing to stop his fall he hit the ground hard, banging his head on the rough terrain underneath him.

"Argh fuck it! Fuck this shit" he reacted angrily. "Daisy where the fuck are you – damn it woman".

Picking himself up and brushing off the leaves and dirt from his jeans, he turned around to be greeted by the sickening site of Daisy's motionless body sprawled at the stump of a tree.

Her stomach was ripped wide open and her insides spewed across her body. Her face was badly disfigured from something that seemed sharp but with each slice more brutal than the last. Blood was covering a large portion of her body so the true extent of her injuries couldn't be seen.

What was more noticeable was that she had been strapped to the base of the tree by what looked like old chains that had been wrapped around her neck. This was no animal attack that was for sure!

Turning away in fear, he felt a sudden punch to his stomach and then a piercing pain running through his upper torso. Blood exploded out from his mouth and he felt a tugging sensation, like something was being removed from his body. Trying to catch his breath and in complete shock, he instinctively went to cover his stomach with his hands. Then came another blow to the same area. This time the sharp object went even deeper and sliced through both hands severing several fingers at the same time.

Kneeling to the ground he looked up to see a huge bulking figure standing over him. Wearing a deep red and black tartan looking shirt and blue workman's overalls that where filthy, presumably from time spent in the forest, the figure was also wearing some sort of mask.

But none of this was of any consequence. The pain was becoming too intense now and he was starting to go cold very quickly, his senses seemed scrambled and all over the place. Looking down at the wounds and the blood-stained remains of his hands he could no longer do anything to protect himself. With dizziness now starting to affect his balance he fell forwards, head first on to the damp forest floor.

Standing over him and with a bloodied axe in both hands, the figure raised it high above his head and without hesitation he rained down heavy blows, one after the other onto the now lifeless body.

12

Rummaging through her backpack Jessica heaved a sigh of relief and pulled out a can of alcohol, amongst the other contents of her overly stuffed bag.

Mark was quick to point out that they all had a long weekend ahead of themselves and he didn't want any hangovers or individuals slowing the other members of the group down.

"Yeah, erm, guys – if you could keep the alcohol consumption to a bare minimum tonight please, we've got a big trek ahead of us tomorrow." he said, objecting at Jessica choice of beverage.

Unimpressed, Jessica shook her head making it clear he was not in charge of events this weekend. "Whatever Mark, when did you lose your balls?" she said.

"Maybe we should try and phone Bruce again, it's going to be getting dark soon" Pamela interrupted. She could sense a possible row erupting between Mark and Jessica so was quick to change subject. "Maybe he's just got cold feet" replied Jessica.

"Well its official, there's no signal out here and what the fuck am I supposed to do these next two days?" Kirsty had been wandering around the campsite trying to find the best location for a signal on her mobile but to no success.

"How are we supposed to get hold of Bruce now?" Pamela asked.

"Err, don't look at me, I didn't invite him to this party" Mark responded with little sympathy.

Annoyed that no one seemed to be taking her seriously, Kirsty tried again to get the others attention. "Do we really have to stay here, it's disgusting!" she whined.

Taking the bait, Jessica was quick to respond. "Looks like you girlfriend doesn't like the great outdoors Mark."

"Maybe you like slumming it in the mud Jessica but some of us have class!" Kirsty replied as tensions rose.

Taking a few shortcuts through the dense forest, Bruce wasn't too far behind the rest of his friends. He couldn't wait to meet up with

Jessica and Pamela again, it had been a long time since they last met in Aberdeen. It was to celebrate Pamela's new job since leaving university and so he and Jessica had arranged a surprise night-out.

With his mind focused on meeting up with them he didn't notice the chain laying across the pathway until it was too late. Hitting the breaks on his bike, momentum took him past the point of no return, his front wheel becoming entangled and locked and throwing Bruce from the bike.

Tumbling over the bicycle, Bruce hit the floor hard. Slowly, he tried to sit himself up, holding his ribs in the process. He was hurt but nothing more serious than being winded and perhaps a few bruises to show in the morning.

Sitting there he was sure the chain had been pulled in the last seconds before his bike hit it. "No, that can't be possible" he tried to convince himself.

"Are you trying to fucking kill me" he screamed out. Looking through the dense forest for any sign of someone messing about.

Getting to his feet and rubbing the back of his neck, he noticed the front wheel on his bike was now buckled.

"Shit!" he mumbled to himself. Suddenly, the sound of branches being snapped could be heard from close by as if someone or something was walking on them.

"HELLO?" he shouted out and the sounds instantly stopped. "HELLO!"

The sound of snapping twigs appeared again but not wanting to see what was making them, Bruce dropped the now useless bike onto the ground and began to set off walking in the opposite direction.

Making his way further into the forest and all the time keeping his focus directly on what was in front of him, he didn't dare look behind as fear was now playing tricks with his mind. He was now convinced that someone definitely did pull the chain making his bike flip over and if that was the case then what was their intention?

The noises coming from the forest where getting much louder with each step Bruce made. Someone was definitely following him that's for sure but he needed to get his breath back. Stood in the middle of the forest and with no clue as to how close he was to the campsite, Bruce tried to stay quiet so not to alert whatever or whoever was following him.

It had gone quiet. But only for a short period. Suddenly the strange noises reappeared but this time it seemed they were much closer than before and now they were also in front of him. Bruce was being circled. Possibly hunted!

Not wanting to hang around for too long, Bruce backtracked to try and find a clearing in the forest. It was now starting to get dark and he knew he wasn't alone in these woods.

To gain some momentum Bruce went from a fast pace walk to running within a few seconds when suddenly and without warning his foot gave way on the loose fodder on the ground.

Pulling himself up off the muddy gravel, he paused for a brief moment and stared intently at the view in front of him. It was quiet – apart from the sound of the wind rustling through the leaves on the trees. The strange sounds he was fearing had seemingly stopped.

Trying to find some composure, Bruce leaned forwards, hands on his knees as he tried to catch his breath again – he hadn't noticed the figure maneuvering into position behind him and without any warning, the figure took a right-swing with his fist and caught Bruce full on the side of his face, knocking him unconscious to the ground. The force of the punch was so strong that it caused blood to slowly creep out from Bruce's ear.

Helpless, Bruce could do nothing to stop the figure from grabbing him by the clothes on his back, dragging him up from the floor and effortlessly heaving his body over his large frame.

Pamela had strayed just out of view of the others – wandering around looking for any signs of Bruce. She had a feeling that something was wrong as it wasn't like him to be late to any event. He was usually the first to arrive and this was out of character.

"BRUCE" she shouted out as she walked tentatively through the forest. "BRUCE. BRUCE WHERE ARE YOU?"

Stopping to check her phone, she noticed she had a signal, albeit a low signal. Quickly finding Bruce on her contact list she dialed his number.

In the distance a phone started to ring – it was Bruce's. He *had* been close to the group after all!

Keeping the phone to her ear she tried to locate where Bruce's phone was ringing from and slowly made her way in the same direction. Taking short steps, she followed the ringtone.

Moments later she found Bruce's phone. Why it was left on the ground she didn't know but she was now more certain than ever before that something was seriously wrong.

Rushing back to her friends, Jessica was the first to greet her.

"You alright Pamela?" she quizzingly asked.

"We seriously need to consider heading back." replied Pamela.

Looking concerned, Jessica stood up and walked over to her, "What's wrong?"

"It's Bruce's phone, I found it out in the woods" Pamela replied, lifting the phone up and showing the group.

Not showing any concerns, Mark shrugged – "Oh so you've found his phone, big deal. At least we know he's out there, somewhere" he said in a mocking tone.

"This is serious Mark, what if he's had an accident or something!" replied Pamela.

"Look, nobody has had an accident. I'm sure he just dropped it whilst out looking for us." Mark still wasn't convinced Bruce was in any trouble.

"Well I'm not just gonna sit here and wait for it to get too dark, we need to look for him or try and at least do something!" Pamela fumed.

Looking at each other, it seemed no one was up for wandering around the woods.

"Well don't look at me, I ain't moving" replied Kirsty with a tone of discontent in her voice.

Storming off in the woods, Pamela was furious with her friends for not wanting to help. She was certain Bruce was in trouble and he wasn't playing any jokes on the rest of them.

"Bruce" she shouted. "Bruce, are you OK?"
Running to catch up with her, Jessica pulled Pamela's arm as if to slow her down.

"Pamela wait - we must have just missed him. He knows we are heading to the house; he probably just went straight there." she said.

"No, somethings not right" replied Pamela.
Feeling helpless but also realising it would be irresponsible for them to be wandering around the woods in the dark, Jessica tried to

compromise with Pamela, "Were gonna have to head back but we'll catch up with him in the morning – I promise".

"I hope he's ok." replied Pamela. Jessica was right, there was nothing more they could do at this point.

13

An hour had passed since Pamela went out into the woods to try and find any sign of Bruce. She had spent most of the time staring at the phone she had found but Bruce had password protected it. She felt helpless and couldn't stop worrying about what had happened to him and why his phone would be left lying on the ground. Meanwhile, Jessica was trying her best to convince her he would be fine by saying he probably dropped the phone by accident and didn't know himself he had lost it until he got to the farmhouse.

"Stop your worrying, Pamela. Like I said, he will be sat around a fire right now, probably drinking and thinking about meeting up with you tomorrow. Two love birds back together again." she laughed.

"I hope so Jessica. I really do hope so. But I just can't stop worrying about him. I just have this horrible feeling something isn't right." replied Pamela.

Meanwhile, Mark – who was leaning over the camp fire he had started earlier, was roasting some marshmallows on sticks. "Aye, everything will be alright." he said.

"So, how far is the house from here?" Pamela asked, hoping someone from the group had a bit more knowledge of the area than she had.

"It should be an hour or so walk, straight down that path" replied Mark pointing directly in front of him. Getting up from his chair, he slowly strolled around the fire looking into the pitch blackness of the woods. "You know, I'm surprised we haven't seen any more party goers by now." he commented.

"Maybe the evil farmer got them" Jessica replied in a mocking tone. "Back from the dead for one last kill!"

Kirsty who was sitting alone and away from the rest of the group looked on, scanning the woods and listening intently to the conversations going on. Although she had relaxed a little and was less stressed than she was a few hours earlier, she still felt uncomfortable towards her surroundings and wished she was elsewhere.

Interruptingly, she managed to force her way into the conversation - "Do you guys know the real story of what happened out here – or are you just as thick as the rest of the people in town?"

"I think we all know the Redwood story" replied Jessica, and it was true that many of the local towns people had indeed heard the story of the Redwood killer as Pamela was quick to verify. "Yeah, I don't think it's something you can easily forget, especially when it involves kids being killed."

Shaking her head and sighing, Kirsty carried on with her own version of the story. "I'm not talking about what mummy and daddy told you to keep you out of these parts of the woods. I'm talking about the version no one wants you to know about, what really happened." she replied.

14

Friday, July 7th, 1972

14:32pm

It had been another couple of sleepless nights for the farmer. The dreams he had been having had intensified since his encounter with the presence two days previously but he never spoke to his wife about what happened that early morning. He didn't want to frighten or put any stress or extra burden onto her and he was also worried for his children and didn't want to scare them with tales of monsters or strange goings on in their home.

The day had started like any other morning and he had already started working in the fields by the time his wife and children where awake. He'd been out chopping down trees and repairing some damaged fences that had been uprooted and blown over by the storm that passed over their farm two days ago. Whilst it was a moderately normal storm, it was still powerful enough to cause some damage that needed tidying up.

The weather was humid with hardly any breeze and it was too hot to be working outside but jobs needed doing and he didn't want to be inside his home anyway – not with recent events still very much fresh in his head.

He had already started chopping the fallen trees when seemingly out of nowhere the noise of children laughing could be heard. Looking up from the axe that he had planted into the stump of a tree, he turned his head so he was facing into the direction of where the laughing was coming from. In the distance there was a clearing in the woods and thinking it could be his two children playing he gazed ahead for a few seconds.

"Hello?" he shouted. "Kids, is that you?"
Not getting a response he carried on looking into the clearing, occasionally looking around in other directions in the hope of catching a glimpse as to who was making the laughing sounds.

"Stop messing me about!" he shouted out.
The laughing continued but the more he shouted for it to stop the louder and more intimidating it became.

Taking hold of the axe, he made his way into the direction of the laughing before turning slightly away towards the clearing where the woodland started to merge.

Suddenly the laughing stopped, to be replaced by a young child's plea. "Please daddy. Kill them. Kill them all." it said.

Quickly turning around the farmer became anxious and the realisation that he was not alone quickly started to sink in.

"Bury them. Bury them all." came the voice again.

"Stop it. STOP IT" the farmer screamed out. "LEAVE ME ALONE!" he shouted.

The laughing continued but this time it was much louder.

"Daddy. Come with us" came one voice, his daughters voice!

The farmer spun around and in front of him stood his daughter.

"Morgan?" he asked. "Morgan, why are you here? Why have you been playing silly games with me? And where is your brother"

Morgan turned around and started to walk away from her father, unperturbed by his questions.

"Don't walk away from me!" he shouted. "Morgan, did you hear me? Do not walk away from me!"

By this time Morgan had made her way into the woods, ignoring her father's demands and knowing that he would follow her she started to playfully skip over the fallen bracken and twigs that covered the woodland floor.

Puzzled by his daughter's strange behaviors, he proceeded to follow her into the woods but no matter how fast he walked, it felt like she was always a couple of feet further in front and no matter how faster he went he was never going to catch up with her. "Slow down, Morgan – slow down!" he shouted.

It didn't matter. Morgan was too far in front of him and she was disappearing further into the woods which had by now become much denser and trickier to maneuver through. He was now being cut on the hands and face by the sharp thorny bushes and thistles that populated the untouched areas of the woods as well as occasionally falling over on the uneven surface.

Stopping for a short intake of air the farmer had now lost sight of Morgan. He knew it was futile to even try and shout out her name and he couldn't understand why she was ignoring him. It wasn't like her to act this way and it certainly wasn't like her to be in these parts of the woods alone as she was always taught to keep out of these places.

Stumbling on through the woods and after spending more time on the floor than actual walking, he could finally see a parting of the trees and through them the gold colored glint of barley swaying in the summer breeze. He had managed to find the edge of the woodland and yet somehow, he had also lost sight of Morgan. Despite several attempts at shouting out her name he never got a response back.

Making his way into the field, the laughing he had heard a short while ago returned but this time without wanting to provoke the menacing laughter, he tried his best to ignore it. In the distance he saw what looked like a scarecrow - which isn't an uncommon sight in fields like these – but he felt like he was being drawn to it, like he had to go over to it for some specific reason.

The scarecrow was unlike others he had seen or like the ones he used to make with his children. This one was perched on what looked like a make-shift cross, covered with an old shirt that had soil and other stains impregnated into it. The big difference between this scarecrow and the ones generally found in fields like these was this one didn't have any straw or other fillings associated with it. Just a cross with a tatty old shirt placed over it. This just didn't seem to look like a scarecrow solely for the purpose of keeping birds away from the crops.

But it was the mask that stood out. The mask was something that he had never seen before. Covered in a thin layer of dust, it seemed to have been made from some form of hessian, a rough cloth of sorts that resembled that of jute or hemp. The eyes had been stitched with such precision that both had three thick layers of strands covering where the eye sockets should be. The mouth seemed to be absent apart from a slight indentation that gave the illusion that it was breathing by itself. Maybe it was the slight breeze that was causing the mask to look alive but the farmer could not break away from its gaze.

Standing there the farmer stared into the mask – everything around him now disappearing into a haze as he became transfixed with the effigy that was in front of him. Suddenly, the summer breeze and the solitude of the barley fields where replaced with images of crows filling the now darkened skies and a searing heat that seemingly came from nowhere. The scarecrow was no longer in front of the farmer, instead replaced with a hideous looking character that resembled a man, covered in blood with scarring to his face and what looked like burn marks to his hands. Standing there, the farmer could not break himself away from the intense gaze this 'thing' was directing at him, transfixed to the images that where flooding into his mind. Just like he had witnessed days previously, he was seeing bodies lying strewn around the fields - decapitated, arms and legs cut off and left to rot with the crows feasting on the corpses.

"You have to kill them all." The farmer could hear a voice coming from the figure in front of him. "All. Kill them all!" it demanded.

The hold that the figure had over the farmer was slowly waning and he was starting to regain some consciousness by the time the images in his head had started to wane. But the figure was still there – taunting him.

"You have no need for them, any of them" it spoke. The farmer blinked, once, twice and on the third blink he managed to lower his head to rub his eyes. Looking back up he was stunned to find that the figure was now replaced by something more unimaginable – an exact replica of himself!

Without any heeding or any warning, the thing lurched itself forwards towards the farmer and just like that – it was gone.

Snapping back into what he perceived as reality, the farmer found himself stood alone in the barley fields, the summer breeze silently blowing onto his face and the sound of birds in the trees in the near distance all grouped together. The childish laughing had stopped, the images had gone and everything seemed back to normal – except *he* felt different.

As confusion came over him, the farmer slowly turned around raising his hand in the process. A crazed expression appeared on his face as he stared at the axe he was still holding.

15

"So, what you are trying to tell me is that he was driven mad by some evil voices?" chirped up Jessica whilst holding just one of a couple of a marshmallows she had prepared earlier, over the camp fire. "How original." she laughed.

"That's not the end of the story, smartarse" replied Kirsty. "Not least the way you idiots think it is anyhow."

Mark looked at Pamela with a smirk on his face to which Pamela started to chuckle. Jessica not wanting to miss out on potentially poking fun at Kirsty couldn't contain herself.

"So, what happened next – Kirsty? Please do tell us." she said.

"If all you're going to do is make fun of me, Jessica, then why should I bother. Why don't YOU tell us all what the real story is?" replied Kirsty.

Mark and Pamela sat watching the unfolding drama taking place, seemingly amused that both Kirsty and Jessica can wind each other up with the smallest of whims.

"C'mon guys, it's just a story – nothing to get into an argument over" Pamela said. "Lighten up the both of you."

Meanwhile, Mark had sat up from his chair to take the kettle pot he had filled with water off and away from the camp fire. "Anyone else want a drink? Tea or coffee!" he asked.

"Tea or coffee. Really Mark? Is that all you have to offer?" asked Jessica. "We are out here camping and all you have to drink is tea or bloody coffee?"

"Like I said earlier, let's keep the alcohol to a minimum. We need clear heads for the walk tomorrow if we are to find the Redwood house" he replied.

"Here Mark – catch!" Jessica responded whilst throwing a tin towards Mark. "Does anyone else want something a little stronger than tea or coffee?" she laughed.

"I'm fine Jessica. Coffee would be nice though Mark" Pamela said in a sheepish manner. She didn't want to come across as 'being boring' as Jessica put-it.

"And what about you, Kirsty – a boring drink or something a little stronger?" Jessica asked.

"How about I just carry on with the story" replied Kirsty.

"Suit yourselves. You enjoy your drinks. And Kirsty, please do carry on with your story, I'm sure it'll keep us all amused". Jessica could be ruthless with her sly digs and knew which buttons to press when talking to Kirsty.

16

Friday, July 7th, 1972

16:50pm

It was mid-afternoon when the farmer arrived back at the farm and the warm air that had been his companion for the best part of the day had since been replaced by a much cooler breeze. His wife was hanging out the few remaining items of clothing that she had been washing for most of the day onto a make shift line that he had crudely erected after the recent storm had brought down the original pole during the night.

Standing there he watched as she took pegs from a home-made peg bag and placed a towel on the line. As the wind blew the towel to-and-fro, she noticed that he was watching but didn't think anything unusual of this.

"Hello love. Have you finished the repairs on those fences?" she asked him, bending down to take another piece of clothing from the pile and then hanging it next to the towel. Not getting a response she drew back the towel to get a clearer view of her husband.

"Are you ok? You seem quiet." She paused for a few seconds. "Is everything alright?" Feeling a little uneasy she got the sense something wasn't right.

Without saying anything, the farmer started walking towards her, his face contorted with a maniacal expression. He was still holding the axe that he had been using throughout the day, sunlight reflecting off the sharp but worn edge.

Feeling threatened she turned to try and get away from her husband but in doing so her right foot caught the laundry basket on the ground. Losing her footing she couldn't help herself from tumbling to the ground with her left hand taking the brunt of the impact with an instant pain shooting through her lower arm and wrist.

Managing to sit herself up, she lifted her left arm to see her wrist was out of place. The pain was getting much stronger and a sense of sickness was fluctuating between that and dizziness. But that was the least of her worries as she knew she had to get away from her husband.

Looking up from her hand she couldn't see where he had gone. He was no longer in view. Panicking, she managed to get back onto her feet but just as quickly as her husband had disappeared, there he was – standing within a couple of feet of her, the clothes on the washing line blowing around his head. He had a chilling grin on his face – a strange kind of look that she had never seen from him before.

She never had time to react as a quick swing of his axe tore into her abdomen. Once again, she fell backwards onto the floor but this time there was no getting back up. He raised the axe above his head, bringing it down onto her chest with such force it cracked open her rib cage, exposing glimpses of her internal organs with blood oozing out and onto her now ripped clothes. With the limited energy she had left she raised her broken hand towards her husband who was readying himself for another swing of the axe.

Bringing it down one last time, the axe sliced through her hand and into the remains of her already butchered body. As he stood above her now helpless body, he tried wiping some of her blood away from his face, but in doing so he could taste the sweet stickiness of it as it touched his lips. Holding both his hands up he saw that they were both covered in blood but this only made him more curious. Slowly, he placed an index finger into his mouth, licking the blood off it, followed by the palm of his hand and then the rest of his fingers.

Animalistic traits came over him and just as a vulture would circle over a dead carcass readying itself for a feast, he looked down upon his wife's bloodied body but instead of waiting for his prey to die, he knelt down at the side of her – running his hand over the open wounds that he had made only seconds ago. Picking at some of the flesh that was now hanging loose, he tore small parts away and placed them into his mouth. The more he tasted the bigger the pieces of flesh they became. This was more of a starter than a main course as he turned his gaze into the slow beating organs that were now clearly visible. The main course was now ready.

17

The farmers children had been playing in fields at the opposite side of the farm and had been having fun for most of the afternoon, chasing each other, playing hide and seek and at times lazing around enjoying the hot sun beating down on them. They didn't get too much time to play as children as they often had chores to do around the farm when they were not attending the local school but today was different, the school was closed due to the storm and a lot of the damage that needed fixing around the farm was easy enough for the farmer to do on his own so the children were allowed to have a rare day to themselves.

Morgan was the eldest with Jacob, her brother, being a year and a half younger. But they both looked out for each other and if one got into any trouble then the other would stand up for them – Morgan usually being the one to do the standing up!

During the afternoon Jacob had managed to get his shoes dirty whilst running close to the edge of a stream and knowing his parents would be cross with him if they saw the state of the shoes, he had told Morgan to set off walking back to the farm on her own so he could try and clean them up with some water from the river. It was only a couple of minutes' walk back to the farm house and he could at least keep his eyes on her.

As Morgan got closer to the farm house she could see that clothes where still on the washing line in the back yard so thinking her mother was still outside, perhaps ready to bring them in she thought it would a nice gesture to walk around and do that herself and in the process stay in the good books with her parents just in case Jacob gets back with his shoes still muddy.

Making her way around and then entering through an open gate she saw her father on his knees leaning over her mother.

"Father?" she said curiously. "What's wrong with mother?"

By this time the farmer had already sensed someone was close behind him and he had already taken hold of the axe that was now saturated in blood with the stickiness of the fluid gripping hold of mud and grass that had collected from the ground. Slowly making his way to his feet he turned to face his daughter – still chewing on pieces of flesh he had been feasting on.

Shocked by her father's appearance and with a sense of terror coming over her she quickly turned and began to run towards the gate, shouting out her brother's name.

"JACOB!" she yelled. "JACOB, COME QUICKLY – COME QUICKLY, MOTHERS HURT."

Although the farmhouse could be seen from the river Jacob was at, the sound of the water coursing over rocks and trees rustling in the wind made any audible noises from such distances practically impossible to hear.

Knowing she couldn't get to Jacob without her father gaining on her, Morgan turned to the right of the farmhouse in the hope of making it to the only place she thinks will be safe – the barn. The barn was full of places to hide, from stacked bales of hay to darkened corners littered with second hand used furniture that had been collecting dust for generations – this may be her only salvation.

Luckily for Morgan, the door to the barn had been left slightly ajar by the farmer during the morning when he was collecting equipment to do the repairs. Making her way inside she knew she had to be quick in finding a place to hide. There was a ladder in front of her which led to a second floor in the barn. This is where a lot of wood and some old furniture was stored and she and Jacob had played in this part of the barn many times over the years so she knew it quite well.

She had barely found a safe spot by the time the farmer had got to the door of the barn. As she cowered down behind a stack of ply-boards that had been there for years, and with barely enough room to move she managed to sit there, holding both her knees with her hands trying her hardest not to make a sound. She couldn't get the images of her mother lying there on the ground, her father covered in blood. Shaking and with more tears starting to appear she was struggling to contain her heavy breathing.

Below her she could hear her father pushing things over. Large thudding sounds as heavy objects fell to the floor. He was systematically moving things – tools, glass jars, stools, wooden buckets and anything else that was in his way – all crashing down to the floor. Then it went silent. All the noises had suddenly stopped and she couldn't understand why?

Confused, she slowly sat herself up from the crowded corner she was in, managing to peer through an opening in the wooden pieces of wood that were blocking her view. All she could see was the top of the ladder she had climbed to get to the second floor. Suddenly one hand appeared on the ladder and then an axe appeared in the other as the farmers face came into view as he began to pull himself up.

    Panicking, Morgan managed to free herself from the tight corner, running over to the ladder – instinctively kicking her father in his face with enough force he flinched backwards making him lose his grip. Plummeting to the ground the farmer lay there unconscious.

    Outside Jacob had done what he could to try to get most of the mud off his shoes and had made his way back up to the farm unaware of the events that had unfolded with both his mother and sister at the hands of his father. Inside the house everything was quiet and nothing seemed out of the ordinary but as he made his way into the kitchen, he could see the backdoor was slightly ajar, gently hitting the frame as the summer breeze occasionally blew onto it.

    "Morgan, you outside?" he shouted out whilst making his way to the backdoor. "Morgan?"

Not getting a response and blissfully unaware of the sight that was about to confront him, Jacob made his way down the wooden steps leading onto the grass and towards the clothes on the washing lines. As the towels fluttered in the breeze, he caught glimpse of a mass of red and white clothing placed on the floor, the grass also tainted in a dark red colour. Then he saw it, a mangled mess that was once resembled a person, laying there with pieces of flesh ripped away and strewn on the ground. The face was now nothing more than a battered mess with fragments of bone and clumps of hair peeking out from the pulp.

"Mother?" he whispered. His brain was trying to unscramble what his eyes where seeing but instinct was also telling him that this was his mother. "MOTHER!" he screamed out. "MOTHER!"

Back in the barn Morgan was still on the second floor looking down on her unconscious father, too scared to climb down the ladder to make her way to the barn door. She knew she had to get out but her body was frozen with fear.

To the side of her there was a window but this had been boarded up years ago to prevent her and Jacob from having any accidents. Her father knew they liked to play in the barn so he had done his best to make it as safe as possible. Not wanting to climb down the ladder she slowly made her way to the window and started to pull on the wooden struts in the hope a batten or two may be loose which could make a gap just wide enough for her to climb through and onto the roof below.

Some of the wood had deteriorated over the years and it didn't take long for a couple of the struts to come loose. Pulling them away, Morgan had enough room to squeeze through the narrow gap and make her way outside. Taking a look over the edge, the drop below her was maybe three to four metres high but the ground below was soft enough to break her fall. Fearing her father would be awake soon and without giving it much thought she turned her body around slightly just enough to half lie on the roof with her legs dangling over the edge. Inching her body down and over the roof and with a loose grip on the guttering, she was about to let go when suddenly she caught sight of her father from the corner of her eye. He had become conscious and made his way back outside of the barn!

Panicking, Morgan scrambled to try and lift herself back up onto the roof but there wasn't anything other than the gutter to get hold of. Screaming for help and trying her best to climb back up, she lost grip in both hands and plummeted to the ground below her.

Her father was only a few feet away from her by the time she hit the ground but dazed and slightly winded Morgan tried to pull herself up. It was too late. Her father was too close and by the time she could react he was already looming over her, his face contorted with anger.

"Daddy. Daddy, please – don't hurt me" she cried out.

Lurching forwards, her father took hold of her wrist, forcibly dragging her up off the floor. He never said anything – he didn't need to as he turned away and started walking towards the barn. Morgan struggled to keep up with him, falling to the ground on numerous occasions – all the time her father just grunting each time he had to drag her back up and onto her feet.

"Daddy, what are you doing? Where are we going?" she tried asking but he remained silent.

Just outside of the barn, Morgan noticed an old tree stump with an axe planted firmly into it and the awful realisation that this could be where her father was dragging her to started set in.

Panicking, she started to dig her feet into the ground in the vain hope of slowing her father down but his grip on her wrist got tighter and tighter each time she stumbled to the floor.

Fearing for her life she started to scratch her father's hand, digging her nails deep into his skin. Stopping for a moment, he glanced over at his daughter and noticed the blood that had started to appear from the scratches. In a fit of rage, he threw her to the ground and with a swing of his left foot he kicked Morgan in the stomach with such force she could hardly breath.

The axe was only a couple of feet away and with Morgan now lying on the floor and in severe pain, the farmer managed to reach over and grab it. Standing over his daughter, he lifted the axe above his head and in one quick motion he brought it down with such force and savagery he decapitated her head from her body – the axe planting itself firmly in the ground below.

18

"I knew he killed his kids, but eating his wife – that's messed up!" Pamela said with a look of repulsion on her face. Meanwhile, Mark and Jessica both sat there, listening intently at the story Kirsty was telling.

"And it gets a lot worse. The official report said that they found the farmer's son, in a shallow grave, stabbed repeatedly. The farmer himself, he was eventually found dead. Sick fuck took his own life and hung himself."

Laughing to herself, Kirsty put out a cigarette she was smoking and finished off the story. "Funnily enough, it was around here – somewhere, where he did it" she said. "Anyway, but what the authorities didn't want anyone to find out about and what you don't know is that they NEVER found the boy's body, the grave was completely - empty."

By this point Pamela, Jessica and Mark were engrossed in the tale being told by Kirsty, with all of them sitting in complete silence.

"Legend has it that his tormented soul came back from the dead – an evil entity hell bent on killing anyone or anything that dare disturbs the resting place of his butchered family." Kirsty continued.

With everyone now fully taken in by the story and all completely silent, Kirsty let out a loud yell to scare them – each one of them jumping in their make-shift seats.

Everyone burst out into a nervous laugh with Mark holding onto his chest. "You should've seen your face!" he said to Jessica.

Trying not to laugh, Pamela replied in an unconvincing tone "Very funny guys!" whereas Jessica tried to put a tougher expression on. "You're honestly pathetic, both of you." she said whilst throwing a marshmallow she had been holding, into the camp fire.

"So, did you just make all that up?" Pamela asked Kirsty.

"Well that's just what my mum tells me every anniversary of the murders." she replied.

Mark had relaxed a little by now and tried to be more logical than the others. "It's obviously just a story your mum tells you just so you don't go walking in the woods." he said.

"Ok Mark," Kirsty replied. "As you seem an expert on this, why don't YOU tell us your version?"

"Aye, well it's a little tamer than yours Kirsty. Not as gruesome as you make out anyways."

Leaning over to pull out a beer from his backpack, Mark sat back in his chair and opened the can. Taking a sip, he looked at the rest of his friends who were all looking upon him, waiting to hear his version of events of the murders.

"Come on Mark, were waiting." Pamela chuckled.

"Well the murders certainly took place, we already know that, but there was nothing paranormal about them, no scarecrow or possession as you make out Kirsty. Nah, nothing like that." he continued.

"So, what then, he just went nuts and slaughtered his entire family for no reason?" Kirsty said.

"No, I'm not saying that." Pausing, he looked around at his friends. "Look, the story I got told was that secret experiments took place somewhere around these parts using ex-military men. Some kind of hormone enhancing drugs that made them much stronger than the average soldier. The experiments only last a few months until they were shut down for being unethical. The MOD got involved and those behind it where put under military arrest. That's it!"

"And the soldiers who were being tested on, what, they were just allowed to leave and lead normal lives?" Kirsty mockingly asked. "Yeah, right!"

"I don't know what happened to them. Perhaps they were allowed to leave. I don't know." replied Mark. "Anyway, that's the version I was told and it was one of these soldiers that went on to own the Redwood house before going on to murdering his family. Perhaps the drugs had taken their toll on him and he didn't know what he was doing?"

Not too impressed with his story, Kirsty stood up to stretch her legs and take a walk towards the camp fire. It was getting colder and the heat the fire was giving off felt like heaven to her. "Well that wasn't scary at all Mark." she said unamusingly, warming her hands close to the fire. "What about you Pamela? Do you have a different version of events? What's your take on the Redwood killer?" she asked.

Pamela had never given it much thought, although she had heard plenty of tales over the years from family and friends. To her, the murders where brutal and shocking but nothing that didn't seem out of the ordinary in today's society. The world is a scary, crazy place and things like this are now common place in the news.

"It was a Bodach that killed them!" she said in a light hearted tone.

"A what?" Mark asked.

"A Bodach – a bogeyman!"

"A bogeyman? Really, is that that best you got?"

"Yeah, well its better than a bloody scarecrow or secret experiment. Everyone is scared of the bogeyman aren't they! As kids we are told not to be naughty by our parents or else the Bodach would come and get us."

Standing up and holding out his beer, Mark announced - "Well, everybody's got a tale to tell, I guess! So, I propose a toast - to the Redwood massacre and to the evil, demonic boy, or should I say – Bodach! that still lives in these woods."

Seeing the funny side Kirsty was the first to join him. "I'll drink to that!" she stood up and said. "Well, why not" Pamela replied. "Come on Jess, what do you say?"

Not wanting to be the party pooper, Jessica stood up and in unison all of them raised their drinks. "To the Redwood massacre."

19

Mark wasn't fully asleep when he heard the shuffling sound coming from outside his tent. He had struggled to get comfy all night and the tight knit conditions due to the space inside the tent had made for an unbearable night plus it didn't help his cause with Kirsty's constant fidgeting at the side of him.

Slowly sitting up, he took his time not to disturb Kirsty as he crouched forwards and hesitantly opened the zipper on his tent, looking back to make sure she was still asleep as he pulled back the opening and began to crawl out.

In front of him he saw the silhouette of a figure sat in front of a barely lit fire, seemingly warming their hands over the burning ambers. Rubbing his eyes as he slowly made his way over, it became obvious to him who the figure was – it was Jessica of all people. "Oh great!" he muttered under his breath.

"Hey there. You struggling to sleep too?" he asked, keeping his voice low so not to wake Kirsty.

Looking up, Jessica pulled a face as if somewhat disappointed that it was Mark who was stood behind her and not one of her other friends. "You could say that." she replied.

"Shouldn't you be worried if Kirsty catches you talking to me?"

"Nah, she's fast asleep. And anyway, what does she expect us to do? Keep our distance the whole weekend?" replied Mark as he squatted down next to Jessica.

Shaking her head, Jessica smirked a little which made him a little uncomfortable.

"What?" he asked.

"C'mon Mark, you know what she's like. She hate's me and its obvious she doesn't want to be here this weekend. I just don't need the hassle."

"What hassle? She can't stop me talking to other people you-know."

"But I'm not just anyone am I Mark?" Jessica answered back in an abrupt manner.

Reaching his hands over the burning ambers, he took a look over his shoulder at the surroundings and into the darkness of the woods. Taking in the view for a few seconds he could feel a cold chill that was constantly blowing around them.

"Fucking hell its cold." he complained as he put his hands under his armpits to give himself a kind of hug.

"Mard-arse." laughed Jessica.

She was right, he was a mard-arse and he knew it. He'd always been a push-over to his friends and even family members ever since he could remember. People could easily get him to do whatever *they* wanted and he never put up an argument.

"I'm sorry Jess, for everything." he muttered under his breath.

"Mmm!"

"What? I mean it. I'm sorry for shit I put you through."

They both sat in silence, with only the sound of the crackling fire in front of them until Mark continued with his apologies.

"I guess we are just two opposites. You loved the social life and I was always too busy with work. Not that I didn't like being out with your friends but – "

"But what?" Jessica interrupted him.

"Seriously Mark, but what? You hardly ever came out with me, always had an excuse for not wanting to get to know my friends and yes, it was always work before me."

"Hey! I'm sorry, alright! I'm just trying to apologise."

Jessica looked down at her hands that where now glowing from the heat of the fire and started to rub them together to try and circulate some of the heat. Sniffling, she got to her feet as her body shivered.

"Well, it's a bit too late to apologise now Mark. Things have changed. We've all moved on." she replied.

Mark nodded and could accept what she was saying. "Have you ever thought of what we could be doing if only I hadn't – "

"Mark stop! Just stop, alright!" Jessica snapped. "Just drop it. You're with her now so just get on with it. Not that I can understand what you see in her but you made a choice."

At this point, Mark was beginning to feel embarrassed by where the conversation was heading. "Yeah, fair enough. Sorry Jess." he replied.

Out of nowhere Jessica started to giggle to herself, quietly so not to wake the rest of the group.

"Oh, so this is funny is it?" Mark asked, slightly annoyed that Jessica was apparently now finding the situation funny.

"Stop being a twat Mark." she replied back. "I'm laughing at the pig back there that is snoring their head off!" nodding in the direction of Pamela's tent.

Her snoring was quiet at first but Jessica had noticed it had gotten much louder all the time she and Mark had been talking. So loud it was a wonder Kirsty hadn't been woken by it.

"Ahh, good old Pamela!" laughed Mark. "Right, I need to take a pee. You gonna be awake a little longer Jess?"

It was too cold for Jessica and despite how tired she was feeling she knew she would struggle to get any sleep any time soon.

"I guess." she replied.

Slowly making his way around the camp fire, Mark paused for a couple of seconds and turned to see she was rummaging through her jacket as if looking for something.

"Well, I won't be long. Why don't you put some water in the can and I'll make us a hot drink when I get back?" he motioned, pointing his finger at the silver aluminum kettle that was lying on top of Jessica's back pack before he made his way into the darkness of the woods.

20

Not wanting to stray too far into the woods, Mark stopped just out of sight of Jessica and could still see the flickering flames coming from the camp fire, albeit with a slight struggle but nevertheless he could see the orange glow in the distance.

"This'll do." he said to himself whilst unzipping the front of his trousers.

Peering out into the darkness he could just about make out the silhouettes of trees in the distance and the odd few stars that where visible under the canopy of leaves above him.

"Well, it's a good job I don't need to take a shit!" he said to himself as he started to urinate. He was right – this was most definitely not the best time or place to be digging holes!

Suddenly, the noise of someone or something making their way through the dense undergrowth startled Mark. Looking up, he stared into the direction of the sound, trying to focus on anything moving but it was just too dark.

"Hello?" he asked out in a nervous tone. "Bruce? Is that you?"

Everything stayed silent as he continued looking all around him, slowly turning around to face all directions. "C'mon, Bruce – if that's you stop being a dick OK?"

Still nothing.

Pulling up the zipper on his trousers, he'd had enough of feeling spooked and turned to start walking back to the camp site where he was hoping Jessica had hopefully made them both a hot drink.

He hadn't even made his first step before another sound came from the woods but this time it was just in front of him and as before it was just too dark to see anything.

"What the fuck?" he muttered under his breath. "Fuck's sake – man up!"

Plucking up the courage, he began to walk towards the dimly lit fire in front of him, using his hands to feel for any obstructions that could block his way. His eyes had only just started to adjust to his surroundings and just as he felt safe enough to pick up some pace, he slipped on the wet foliage under his feet, falling to the ground onto a mound of muddy decayed leaves and soil that had accumulated over the years.

"Arrgh!" he annoyingly blurted out. "You gotta be kidding me!" as he knelt on his knees, rubbing his hands on his jacket to remove the mess that had no doubt covered them. "What a fucking joke!"

By this time, he hadn't given the strange noises he had heard earlier any further thought, instead wanting to get back to Jessica as quickly as possible.

Getting up onto his feet and giving his hands one final wipe on the backside of his jeans he looked over to the campsite to see a tall figure quickly glance by past the fire. It was too dark to make out any clear indications as to who it was. It seemed too big to be Jessica or Kirsty for that matter but it moved far too quickly to jump to any conclusions.

Mark stood there, in the silence of the darkness, seemingly shaken from what he just saw. He didn't want to shout out in case it was Jessica standing up as this would only wake Kirsty and then all hell would break loose.

For a couple of minutes, or so it seemed, he stood watching from the apparent safety of the woods and nothing further happened. No signs of the strange figure and no further sounds that had freaked him out earlier.

Knowing he couldn't stay out in the woods much longer and with Jessica, Pamela and Kirsty all alone at the camp site, he started to make his way back. It only took him a minute or so but it was obvious something strange had occurred whilst he was taking a pee.

Jessica's backpack was still in the same position with the small kettle still placed on top but he noticed the jacket she was wearing was now on the floor a few feet away from the rest of her belongings.

"What the hell?" he asked himself, picking up the jacket as he looked it over. "Why would you take you jacket off in this temperature Jess?"

Puzzled, Mark looked over to her tent and noticed it was still unzipped. Perhaps she decided to go to sleep after all? Meanwhile, Pamela's and his own tent where both zipped up and he could still hear the snoring coming from Pamela's tent – albeit much quieter than when he last heard her.

"Oh well, I guess it's time for bed then."

Making his way over to Jessica's tent and still clutching at her jacket he was oblivious to the shadowy figure lurking in front of him.

Peering inside her tent, it was becoming pretty clear she wasn't inside. "Jess?" he whispered as he knelt down to feel inside. If she was here, he would be touching her feet by now but he felt nothing. She was gone.

Realizing by now that something wasn't right, he quickly scampered back out of the tent and got onto his feet and even though he was becoming spooked out by the situation he still didn't want to wake either Pamela or Kirsty.

"Fucks sake Jess. Where are you?" he thought to himself. "If she's gone to take a piss why would she leave her jacket behind?"

Then, just as he did when he was taking a pee, he heard the sound of someone walking in the woods just in front of him as fallen twigs and other foliage snapped under the heavy weight that was bearing down on them.

"Mark? Bring over my jacket will you. It's freezing here now." a quietly spoken voice came from the darkness.

"Jess – you frightened the crap out of me!" Mark replied with a sigh of relief. "Why the hell did you take it off in the first place?"

Making his way over to where the voice was coming from, he finally caught up with Jessica who by now fastening the button to her jeans. "Here you go. Are you crazy! Not only is it freezing out here but you fucking scared me!"

"Yeah its cold now but I took the jacket off because I was hot around the fire OK. And then I needed to take a pee. What's the issue? I've only been gone five minutes."

"What's the issue? Well, we're in the middle of who-knows-where in the middle of a freezing cold night for one!"

"And the other?"

"Other what?" Mark replied with a puzzled look on his face.

"Other issue? You said 'for one'" Jessica spoke in a sarcastic tone.

Mark could see Jessica was now poking fun at him and was in no mood. "Stop taking the piss now!" he said.

"Well, I think I've already done that right where I'm standing" she laughed as she pointed down towards her feet.

"Ha Ha – very funny. You'd make a great comedian back in the City. Now come-on, let's get back to the tents before we wake the others up."

Neither of them had noticed another shadowy figure that had been watching them when suddenly a small, flickering light emerged from the darkness a dozen or so meters away from them. Turning to see what or who was causing the light to emerge, Jessica reached out to find Mark's hand, clutching tightly upon doing so.

"Hel – Hello?" she called out. "Mark, what's going on?" she whispered.

Mark had no answer. He was as puzzled as she was right now.

"Hey, who is it? What do you want?" he asked.

The darkness was slowly beginning to give away its secrets as the light from the stranger's hand began to show the features of a middle-aged man wearing some sort of beanie hat and a dark looking coat that made his presence seem much bulkier than what is probably was. It was also now obvious the light he was carrying was that from a cigarette lighter.

"Sorry to scare you guys but can you help? I've been wandering around in the darkness for hours now with no sign of anyone – until now." he spoke with a strong Scottish accent.

"What do you want?" Mark hesitantly asked.

"Nothing much. Just a little help getting out of this hole I'm sort of stuck in."

Mark looked at Jessica as she gestured back at him to go back to the campsite. Mark knew what she meant but he felt obliged to go and help. Shrugging his shoulders, he nodded in the direction of the stranger.

"No Mark! What the fuck are you thinking!" Jessica whispered annoyingly to Mark.

"We can't leave him. If he's struggling, he could hurt himself if he falls over. Who knows what is surrounding him?"

"Jesus Mark. Once a sap, always a sap!"

"I'm not leaving him Jess."

Jessica released her grip on Mark's hand as they both started to make their way over to the stranded stranger. "Just a sec mate." Mark called out. "We'll be with you shortly."

"No rush – I ain't going anywhere too soon." the stranger replied.

Neither Mark nor Jessica noticed it but the stranger was holding another object in his opposite hand to which he was doing his best to keep hidden down to his side. As Mark approached, he tightened his grip. "Hey, what's your name" he asked.

"Mark – and you are?"

The stranger seemed hesitant at first to reveal his name but then replied with an enthusiastic tone, "David. The names David – pleased to meet you."

Mark held his hand out but the stranger didn't seem interested to make acquaintance, instead he seemed to be more preoccupied with Jessica and how far away she was.

"And your friend? What's her name?"

"Oh, that's Jessica" Mark replied, slightly unnerved at the stranger's reluctance to accept his hand.

"Your girlfriend, right?" the stranger quizzingly asked.

"Not anymore she isn't. We have a history but that's about it."

"Yeah, now history and it will stay history!" Jessica had overheard Marks reply and responded with her own.

"Oh, she's lively, isn't she?" the stranger laughingly asked. "A real handful I guess?"

"Aye, you could say that. Just don't piss her off – alright?" Mark warned the stranger.

Both Mark and the stranger looked on as Jessica made her way over to them, struggling to keep her balance on the uneven terrain.

"So, what's the issue, how can we help?" asked Jessica.

"My foot - it seems to be lodged under something down here, not sure what though. Perhaps some old roots? I don't know to be honest."

"Well, we'll soon have you out of there. Come on Jess, give us a lift." Mark beckoned over to Jessica.

Sensing something wasn't quite right with the stranger and feeling a little apprehensive, Jessica stared over at the two tents that both Pamela and Kirsty were occupying. "Perhaps we should wake the others and get them over to help us out?" she motioned by nodding her head.

"Ah forget about them Jess. We can free his foot in no time. Hey mister, you hold onto that tree and I'll try and pull your foot away, OK?" Mark replied as he crouched down to the ground, feeling around for the stranger's foot.

With Jessica's back facing the stranger and with Mark crouched below him, neither of them where aware of the rag that the stranger was holding in his left hand. He had managed to keep it hidden all the time they were talking to him. Without warning, he lifted his hand, placing it firmly over Mark's face, covering his nose and mouth with just enough pressure to leave him breathing in the toxic fumes that had saturated the rag.

Jessica turned around to see the lame fight that Mark was putting up but as she got closer to them, the stranger was physically much stronger and somehow managed to push her over onto the ground, giving the toxic fumes just enough time to make their way into Mark's airways.

Letting go of Mark, his limp body slumped onto the ground with his head falling hard onto some moss-covered rocks. At the same time the stranger quickly lurched over Jessica, kicking her back to the ground for the second time before squatting over her and placing both of his hands around Jessica's throat.

The stranger began to squeeze tightly and then placed one of his hands over Jessica's face and using the same rag as he used on Mark, he applied little pressure until the toxic chemicals began to make his victim sleepy.

A few moments later and with both Mark and Jessica unconscious, the stranger looked over his shoulder at the dimly lit camp fire for any signs of movement from either of the two tents. Neither Pamela nor Kirsty had been disturbed, it seemed, and so the stranger, after getting up onto his feet, peered into the darkness and with a wry smile, he gave out some instructions.

"Get them onto the cart. We don't have room for the others but we'll be fine with these two. And don't make any fucking noise – alright!"

A few yards in front of him stood the hulking presence of another figure. Whatever it was it was huge, perhaps big enough to carry two bodies – one over each shoulder – such was the size of it.

The darkness of the woods had kept this 'thing' well-hidden and out of sight all this time and whatever it was it was used to taking orders.

21

The next morning, Pamela woke to an eerie silence, despite the fact it was still early and everyone, or so she thought, were still asleep - there was an unsettling feeling she couldn't shake off. Unzipping her tent, she peered her head outside and noticed the camp fire from the night before was still lit, albeit ever so slightly. Someone must have been up much earlier to have kept the fire going she thought to herself.

"Guys?" she quietly asked out.

Climbing out of her tent she made her way to the fire, throwing on more twigs and logs that had been set aside by Mark. Still not seeing any movement from any of the tents, Pamela put on her jacket and made her way to Mark and Kirsty's tent.

"Hello, anyone in there?" she asked.

Getting no response and not wanting to possibly disturb them if they were asleep, she went back to the fire, crouching beside it to warm her hands.

With a sense of unease, all she could do was sit there and try to push any crazy thoughts and ideas that she was alone out of her mind but then suddenly, seemingly out of nowhere the noise of snapping twigs could be heard coming from the woods behind her.

Reluctant to turn around she sat there, frozen with fear and not knowing what to do.

"Guys. Guys is that you?" she again asked. Turning her head slowly around to look over her shoulder she couldn't see any of her friends or any noticeable movement in the dense tree line.

"Come on guys, if that's you stop messing me about!" she said whilst slowly getting to her feet. Picking up some courage Pamela started to walk into the direction of the noise she had heard.

"If this is some kind of joke it's not funny!" she angrily shouted. "HELLO?"

Making her way back to the camp site it was clearly obvious by now that she was alone. Pamela knew this but was optimistic one of her friends would hear her. "HELLO?" she again shouted.

Suddenly out of nowhere Kirsty appeared from the woods. "What's with all the shouting?" she asked.

Turning around and with a huge sigh of relief, Pamela was so glad to finally see a friendly face. "Ah man am I glad to see you, where the hell have you been?" she annoyingly asked.

"Fresh water!" came the reply as Kirsty held up her flask. "No one else is gonna get it so I thought I will."

Thinking it strange that Kirsty arrived back at the camp site on her own, Pamela was now worried about her other friends. "Well, where is Mark and Jessica?" she asked.

"What do you mean where's Mark and Jessica?" Kirsty replied with a confused expression on her face.

"Well there not in their tents. Or I don't think they are? I would have thought all my shouting would have woken them." Pamela replied.

Kirsty was by now clearly incensed that her boyfriend was somewhere out in the woods with his ex-girlfriend doing who knows what.

"Well where the fuck are they?" Kirsty replied, clearly annoyed.

"I thought they were with you?" came Pamela's confused reply.

"No. I woke up, he was gone, I presumed he had gone for a slash." Pausing for a moment Kirsty started to think there was more to it than she originally thought. "Oh my god, I'm so stupid!" she muttered to herself.

"Look, let's not jump to any conclusions OK. They probably just out looking for you." Pamela said whilst trying to reassure Kirsty.

But it was clearly obvious it would take a lot more to calm Kirsty.

"Oh yeah, sure, a nice romantic walk with his ex-girlfriend. I'm gonna fucking kill him!"

22

The screams from inside where horrific, almost blood curdling and the not knowing of what was going on behind the closed green door made it even worse. Whoever she was, she was in pain and needing help.

Waking up from the sound of the screaming, Jessica found herself chained to a metal cattle cage behind her. Next to her she saw Mark, also bound and with blood oozing from a deep cut to his head. Both had gags placed around their mouths. Panicking from the screaming coming from the other room, Jessica furiously tried to free her hands from the chains that had bonded her to the cages behind her. She didn't know how long she had been kept captive and the last thing she remembered was her and Mark trying to help the stranger.

Facing her on the opposite side sat Bruce, also chained to a wall and with a gag around his mouth. He looked worse than her with more blood covering the upper part of his body and face.

He was awake and was trying to say something but it was nothing more than a muffled sound and he seemed to be nodding in the direction of the green door. Whatever he was saying it was obvious he had encountered something in the forest and had a good idea as to who or what was in the next room.

Suddenly the green door was dragged open and there stood the silhouette of a tall figure. In the darkness it was very hard for Jessica and Bruce to make him out but then he lurched forwards into the light that was shining through the broken timbers from the roof above.

Wearing what looked like filthy, blood stained blue brace overalls and a mud covered red and black checked pattern shirt, whoever he was his face was hidden by a crudely homemade burlap mask – similar to those used to make a scarecrow. It was stained with layers of mud and what looked like dried blood. You could hardly make out his eyes as they were hidden by loose strands that had come away from the mask from years of use.

Then they noticed it – a long wooden hickory styled handled axe, at least a meter in length with the blade dragging on the floor. This was the BODACH – the Redwood killer!

Screaming underneath the gag that was covering her mouth, Jessica tried to wake Mark. It only took her a couple of attempts before he came around, shaking his head as he tried to focus on where the noise was coming from. Excruciating pain was shooting through his head from the knock he got during the night and just like Jessica he couldn't remember too much.

The wound to Mark's head looked a lot worse than those on Jessica and Bruce and blood was still seeping from it, slowly running down the front of his face and into his eyes making it harder for him to see properly. Looking to his right he could just make out that it was Jessica who was trying to get his attention as she pulled on the chains whilst kicking out her legs.

With realisation of the situation he and Jessica found themselves in, Mark tugged on the chains around his wrists, pulling strongly but without any success - all the time being watched by the menacing figure who stood staring at his three captives.

Suddenly, the Bodach started to walk towards them, slowly and with a sense of torment as he dragged the axe slightly behind him. His heavy boots, pounding on the wet floor beneath him, splashing muddy water everywhere.

At this point, Jessica was getting even more frantic, pulling harder than before on the chains which only resulted in her wrist becoming scratched and bloodied. She didn't feel any pain though as adrenaline was now pumping through her entire body.

As the Bodach got closer, the sound of the axe scraping on the floor became louder and more intimidating and none of the captives dared to look up. As he approached, the Bodach paused for a few moments and turned to look at Bruce who had closed his eyes and remained silent up to this point. Standing tall above him, the Bodach took in several deep breaths whilst looking down upon Bruce, making the odd flinching motion with his head like he was deciding on what to do next.

Meanwhile, Jessica who had been crying ever since the figure appeared from behind the green door had by now become a lot louder. Turning around and taking a couple of steps forwards the Bodach lurched over both Jessica and Bruce and after a few seconds had passed he raised the axe high above his head, bringing it down hard and with one swoop cutting through the chains that had been bonding Jessica to the cages.

Letting go of the axe, the Bodach suddenly snatched hold of Jessica's hair, forcibly pulling her up off the ground until she was standing in front of him. All the time her hands where still tied together behind her back making any attempt of escape impossible. The Bodach, tall and intimidating, again started to take a few deep breaths before picking her up and tossing her over his shoulder.

Turning his back on Mark and Bruce and with Jessica over his shoulder he made his way to the green door before disappearing into the darkness. Moments later the door slammed shut.

23

Still seething at the thought of Mark and Jessica being alone somewhere in the woods doing who-knows-what, Kirsty had taken the backpacks from Jessica and Marks tents and was hurriedly rummaging through them looking for any clues as to what they may have been up to. Throwing Marks spare clothes out onto the damp ground, she was desperate to find something.

"Kirsty, what the hell are you doing? Those are Marks spares, go easy will you!" Pamela said.

"Fuck Mark and fuck Jessica!" Kirsty snarled back. "If I find anything to say they have both been seeing each other on the quiet then clothes will be the last of his problems."

"Seriously Kirsty, I don't think they have been seeing each other. He seemed happy with you so stop worrying about them being together and let's decide on what we can do now to find out where they AND Bruce are – OK?" replied Pamela.

"There you go, empty, no map!" Kirsty responded whilst throwing Mark's backpack towards Pamela.

Catching it, Pamela took a glance inside. "Shit, what are we going to do now?"

"Do you know the way back home?" Kirsty asked.

Pausing for a short moment and trying to get her thoughts together, Pamela's only answer wasn't going to go down too well with Kirsty. "Look, Mark said the house was only an hour away."

"So!" Kirsty responded quizzingly.

"The party remember? If we can find the house then maybe other campers will know the way back home." Pamela replied.

"And what about Mark and the SLUT?" Kirsty, seemingly unimpressed with the plan couldn't hold herself back.

"Well their gear is still here so they obviously haven't gone too far. Maybe they bumped into somebody else and went to check out the house. I'm sure it's all perfectly innocent."

Pamela could understand Kirsty's frustrations but was also becoming a little tired of her constant sarcastic replies.

"You obviously trust your friend, well I don't" Kirsty quietly replied back.

There was a pungent smell in the room where he had tied Jessica up, a concoction of chemicals – petrol, diesel and other mechanical fluids that mixed with the mold that lined the damp walls that surrounded her. It smelt dirty, toxic even.

He had placed her onto a table with both legs and arms firmly secured with rope. The bloodied gag around her head and inside her mouth prevented her from shouting out and all she could do was cry.

It was dark in the room with hardly any light other than that coming from a few holes in the dilapidated roof above her that shone on some make-shift shelves that held a disarray of rusted old tools, glass jars, chains, ropes and hooks – items that had been used for gods knows what in the past.

Meanwhile, the figure was stood facing away from her, seemingly interacting with items of sorts that he had already arranged onto another table. Gliding his hand across them one by one he was deciding on what to use. Sheep shears, crow bars, iron nips and hammers. Picking up the shears he turned to face Jessica, opening and closing them in a menacing way as if he was gaining some pleasure out of tormenting her. Making his way over to

Jessica she could see what he was holding but powerless to do anything all she could do was turn her head the other way.

Holding the shears over her head, he again menacingly flinched them open and closed before slowly running them down over her body, passing over her breasts and down to her groin. Teasing her, he took hold of her shirt, gripping the bottom of it and snipping off the one fastened button leaving the white vest she was wearing now fully visible. Moving the shears below the vest, he started to cut away at it, making his way back up her torso until the vest was completely cut in half and leaving nothing but her bra exposed.

Still crying, Jessica was now starting to breath more heavily with fear. She had already consigned herself to the worst that could happen to her. Despite her best efforts at trying to wriggle free, the ropes around her wrists and ankles where far too tight.

Turning away from her, the figure turned and walked away, throwing down the shears and scouring the table for another object, picking up at first a pair of snips but then changing his mind after seeing a blade that kind of resembled a sickle. This seemed to be the weapon of his choice on more than one occasion as there was blood, some of it still fresh, on the blade and handle. Taking the blade and making his way back to Jessica, he placed it just above her navel whist slowly twisting it around on her skin, careful at this point not to pierce into her stomach. He seemed to be getting some form of satisfaction from toying with her but this didn't seem to be sexual – instead it seemed to be more about domination.

"Please" Jessica tried in vain to scream out. "Please. No." but her voice was barely audible.

The sharp edge of the bloodied sickle slowly penetrated into her stomach as the figure applied pressure to the handle, slowly turning it clockwise and then anti-clockwise as he pushed down.

Blood instantly oozed made its way into her throat, suffocating her with the bubbles slowly foaming in her mouth. Her screaming had stopped and the pain she originally felt was no longer there, like her brain had accepted that this was the end and no longer needed to warn her of impending danger.

With her last breath she turned her head to face her torturer and came to understand that she was just another victim to this sadistic maniac who had no remorse, no feelings – nothing.

Looking down on his victim, the Bodach removed the gag that was covering Jessica's mouth and placed it just underneath her chin. She was barely alive but it didn't matter to him as rage seemingly came over him. Lifting the sickle away from Jessica's body he proceeded to rain down heavy blows onto her abdomen. Once, twice, three times – each blow becoming harder than the last with the sickle shredding her organs to pieces. He was butchering his her. There was no reason to the violence, there didn't need to be. He was in his happy place.

24

They still didn't want to leave the campsite just in case Mark, Jessica or even Bruce came back. Neither of them wanted to admit it but each of them knew they would have to make the decision to leave and go and find their colleagues or worst-case scenario, leave them behind and go and find help elsewhere.

"15 MINUTES!" Kirsty shouted to Pamela from inside Marks tent. "15 MORE MINUTES AND THEN I'M OUT OF HERE!"

"We can't just leave." Pamela replied, but deep inside she knew Kirsty was right. They couldn't stay around much longer. They needed to be proactive and try and find their friends.

"Well you can do what you want Pamela but as soon as I've finished in here, I'm leaving." Kirsty was still looking for the map Mark had been using the day before.

"Well, OK. I guess we should be doing something. Where do you think we should head too? Do we look for the Redwood farm and hope we bump into some other campers on the way?" Pamela questioned.

Shaking her head and out of sight of Pamela, Kirsty tutted. "I don't give a fuck where we go. The Redwood house, La La Land, the Emerald City – I don't care! All I know is that these woods are scaring the crap out of me and my boyfriend has disappeared into who knows where with his ex. So, forgive me if I don't seem overly concerned as to where we go – just as long as we go soon!"

"Ok, Ok. I get your pissed Kirsty but I'm only trying to help," Pamela replied whilst crouching down to look into Mark's tent. "Here, let me see if I can find that damned map. You've been looking now for ages, perhaps a different pair of eyes may help?"

"Ah leave it Pamela. I've looked everywhere, it's not here. It's not in Jessica's tent either. One of them must have taken it with them." Kirsty responded.

Climbing back out of the tent, Pamela went to the now dimmed camp fire that was now burning on the last remaining pieces of wood. Picking up her backpack and flinging it over her shoulder she started walking off into the direction of a nearby flowing stream.

"Where are you going?" Kirsty asked.

"Well, you wanted to leave so come on, no point in hanging around here much longer." Pamela replied.

Twenty minutes into their walk and deep inside the woods, Pamela had taken the lead and was way out in front of Kirsty.

"You know, I have left a lot of expensive clothing back there." Kirsty bemoaned.

"Well, yeah feel free to go back and get them at any time Kirsty."

Without taking breath Kirsty was still seething over Jessica. "Oh, don't worry, I'll be sending Jessica the bill."

Fed up with Kirsty's constant moaning, Pamela stopped in her tracks and looked up at the sky, rolling her eyes in annoyance and with hands on hips. She then looked down at her feet but thought to herself that it would be an impossible task in trying to sweet talk Kirsty so instead took a deep breath and kept quiet.

"THIS IS RIDICULOUS! I MEAN, DO YOU EVEN KNOW WHERE WE ARE GOING OR ARE WE JUST GOING AROUND IN CIRCLES HERE?" Kirsty shouted out. "DO. YOU. KNOW. WHERE. THE. HOUSE. IS." She continued with a mocking tone.

Having enough of Kirsty and her ranting and clearly pissed off and in no mood for anymore, Pamela couldn't hold back any longer. "What do you want me to say? Do you want me to magical say I know where the house is? Because I can't!" she responded.

Clearly shocked by Pamela's outburst, Kirsty backed down but still couldn't resist getting one last dig in. "Well, it's obvious," she said. "You know, this is all Jessica's fault. She's had this planned out from the very beginning."

Turning around and facing Kirsty, Pamela started to walk forwards, not in a confrontational way but it was still enough to make Kirsty take a step back.

"Does it even bother you that three of our friends have gone missing because it sure as hell bothers me." Pamela asked.

Walking away, Pamela headed off back into the direction they had both just come from. She had seen a clearing in the woods not too far from where they were but had ignored it as she felt it wiser to follow the stream downwards in the hope of coming across walkers or campers who may also have come off the beaten track.

"We have just come that way Pamela, why are we going back?" Kirsty asked.

Pamela chose to ignore her question and kept on walking. Huffing and knowing she was being ignored, Kirsty set off behind Pamela and never said another word.

25

Mark tried his hardest to scream out as the Bodach swung his axe down hard on the rusty chains keeping him tied to the cage but just like Jessica and Bruce, the gag inside his mouth was making it difficult to make any sort of communication. As the chains broke and fell to the floor, the Bodach threw the axe to ground, making a terrible pounding sound as it fell close to the feet of Bruce who had turned his head away just so he didn't witness his friend being butchered. That would have been too much to take in.

It wasn't until he heard the sound of the Bodach's heavy boots walking away that he knew Mark was still alive and being taken into the same room as Jessica. Mark tried to resist but the Bodach had overwhelming power over him and even if he did get free, where was he going and far would he get? This was Marks brain screaming at him but in this moment, he knew he was powerless to do anything.

Realising now that Mark was going to face the same fate as Jessica, Bruce started to pull and tug at the restraints holding him to the metal cage. At this point he didn't care about the pain and the cuts being made to his wrist – he just needed to get free. Pulling down hard with his right hand, the rope holding him started to loosen just enough that with one final tug he could be free. Tearing at his skin and with pieces of flesh protruding around the base of his knuckles, the rope finally came away leaving Bruce with one free hand – enough to hopefully un-tie the other despite feeling excruciating pain.

Whatever was going on in the other room god only knew but Bruce could hear Mark's pleas for help from the pain he was encountering at the hands of the Bodach but there was nothing he could do to help. Numb with fear, Bruce untied his other hand and then noticed the axe of the floor. Leaning forwards, he picked it up and managed to make it onto his feet, his head pounding and his hands in a lot of pain. He was in no state to take on the Bodach but he couldn't leave Jessica and Mark in the other room despite his initial fear.

Inching his way forwards and with agonizing pain running through his body he could still hear Mark pleading for his life. What was going on in the other room? What was the figure doing? Crazy thoughts started to enter Bruce's head and he stopped within a couple of feet of the door. Taking in his surroundings he took a few seconds to try and clear his thoughts but this just made things worse. He didn't know where he was. He didn't know any quick routes to go down or any hiding places should he need them. But it was the fear of what he would see in the opposite room that stopped him from going any further. Both his friends where in there, one possibly dead with the other being tortured. That was something he couldn't witness first hand.

In the room opposite, Mark had been strapped to an old wooden chair. His shirt had been torn off and he was naked from the waist up. His shoes and socks had also been removed with both his legs crudely strapped to the chair legs. Blood was oozing from an open wound at the back of his head and was running down the side of his face and onto the gag that was stopping him from talking. At times he struggled to breath as the sweet sticky taste of it congregated inside his mouth which made swallowing difficult.

The Bodach was stood there, just watching as Mark tried rocking on the chair. Then he started to walk around Mark, always making eye contact with his victim.

Mark was trying his best to break free but the ropes around his hands and feet where too tight. He could rock the chair slightly but it was never going to be enough to push himself over.

Then he saw her, Jessica. The Bodach had moved away from his view of the table where she was laying and Mark knew instantly it was her, despite the red soaked clothing and pieces of flesh protruding from her abdomen. Even though the lighting was poor, Mark could just about make out what was once Jessica's face. There were hardly any distinguishing features left as the figure had disfigured her so badly and with such ferocity that this was no longer a person but a butchered corpse.

Screaming beneath the gag and ignoring the fact he could hardly breath, anger had replaced fear inside of Mark.

"YOU BASTARD! YOU FUCKING BASTARD!" he tried to scream loudly, rocking profusely on the chair. "IM GOING TO KILL YOU!"

Not intimidated by Marks protestations, the Bodach carried on slowly walking around the chair whilst still maintaining his focus directly on his victim.

Trying his hardest to break free, Mark was clawing on the frames of the chair where it seemed other people may have been victim to the monster stood in front of him. He was merely adding his own marks to those that were already there. Scratching like a trapped rat in a cage, he suddenly screamed out in pain as one of his finger nails tore away and lifted up off his finger. He could see the soft tissue from the nail bed with blood seeping out. The pain was intense and he stopped clawing for a few seconds to try and ease some of the pain.

"Please, just let me go," pleaded Mark. "Please."

The Bodach stood and watched for a few seconds before turning away and walking towards a badly lit area of the room. Mark couldn't see what he was doing until the figure turned around and started walking back towards him and then he saw what he was holding.

The Bodach started to the lift it high in the air as he approached Mark and with one quick swoop, he brought the heavy sledgehammer down hard on Marks left knee, shattering the bones instantly into several pieces. The pain was unimaginable as he clasped hard onto the chair arms with both hands. He didn't see the Bodach lift the sledgehammer again, readying himself for another swing and then just as quickly as he raised it, he brought it crashing down onto the right knee, with more force than the first time. Jagged pieces of broken bone protruded through Marks pants as he sat there quivering from the pain.

Mark could barely open his eyes, nor did he want to at this point, with the Bodach yet again raising the sledgehammer for a third time before crashing it down onto the right leg, breaking more bones and causing Mark to shunt backwards on the chair, momentarily passing out.

By the time he came around, the Bodach had exchanged the sledgehammer for a hacksaw that, like many of his other tools, looked used. It was rusty with signs of dried blood on the handle and blade.

Standing behind him, the Bodach lifted Mark's head up and with intimidating intent slowly lifted the saw so Mark could see what he was holding. Having no energy left and knowing he had no chance of escape; Mark had accepted his fate.

The first slice was the worst, the most painful, and as the Bodach started to saw into his scalp, Mark had lost all hope of escaping. It wasn't the way he expected his life to end but here he was and this was it and with each subsequent motion of the saw, Mark's life was slowly ebbing away.

Deciding that he couldn't face the horror of what was going on in the room opposite, Bruce headed off back towards another sliding door behind him. He heard the pain and suffering Mark was encountering and whether or not it was a lack of courage or selfishness, Bruce couldn't bring himself to go and help his friends.

26

It had been sometime since the screaming had stopped. Bruce had navigated a couple of darkened rooms that seemed to connect themselves via sliding doors. Each room was worse than the other with paint peeling from the walls, cobs webs everywhere, water dripping through the openings in the roof and the smell of mold that had found its way into the small crevasses inside the walls that was permutating all around.

Eventually, the rooms seemed to stop connecting with the final room only having one way in and one way out. Inside there where jars, seemingly hundreds of them, scattered everywhere. On shelving, on the floor, inside makeshift cupboards and wall units and some had even been placed inside a fridge that was no longer connected to any electrical mains. Making his way slowly around the room whilst trying to avoid knocking anything over, Bruce couldn't help but seem curious as to what these jars contained and it didn't take long before he was to find out.

Arriving at the fridge, the door was already slightly ajar but nevertheless he took his time to open it further. Inside he saw dozens of jars, all containing items that were hidden in some kind of thick, dark liquid. Some of the liquid was darker than the others whilst a few jars where half or quarterly full of the stuff.

Removing one of the jars from the fridge he proceeded to take the lid off it, taking his time not to open it too quickly and risk spilling whatever was inside over him. Firmly sealed he tightly gripped the jar with one hand and with the other he managed to prise open the lid.

A pungent smell instantly filled the air making Bruce put his hand to his nose and mouth but it was far too strong and he couldn't help but make retching motions. He didn't have the best gag reflex in the world and this was stomach churning!

Pouring out some of the sticky liquid that was in the jar he saw instantly what was inside – two, perhaps three cut off fingers, the bones protruding from the stumps at the point they were cut off from the hand. There may have been more fingers but the shock of seeing them made Bruce take a step back, dropping the jar onto the soft, muddy ground below. Gaining some composure, he went back to the fridge and took another jar out and repeated the process. A tongue in one jar, a finger with its wedding ring still in place in another but worse still, a cut off penis with the testicles seemingly stuffed together. These jars contained the body parts of the victims the Bodach had held captive over the years.

"My god!" a shocked Bruce said to himself. "This can't be real?"

Having seen enough of the macabre collection of body parts, Bruce made his way back out of the room and into a more brightly lit area, still with the same toxic smell of damp in the air and with the same amount of animal shit on the floor that had mounted up over the years. The decaying walls, ceilings and any furnishings that may have been around where now covered in slime and patches of varying degrees of mold.

To his right and just before the door in front of him he noticed two small windows that seemed to overlook some kind of corridor. The glass panes had since long gone but the frame was still partly intact. Peering through he could see a light of sorts, but whether or not this was natural light he couldn't tell but it could be his savior – a way out!

Making his way out of the room and to his right he saw a wooden door that had at one point in time been bolted shut and a bar of sorts may have been used to keep it from opening from the inside. The bar was still laying horizontal over the door but the catch to hold it in place had deteriorated over the years leaving it balancing loosely onto the door frame. Removing the bar was easy but the door itself was tightly wedged in due to years of abandonment with all kinds of weeds and rotten timber that had reclaimed most of the building.

Forcing the door open just enough to allow himself enough space to squeeze through, Bruce made it into the darkened corridor and slowly started to make his way towards the light. All around him the walls were damp and with rain water dripping from the roof above him everything he touched felt slimy and gross but it was the smell that he had noticed first and foremost. Whilst the other areas of the building he had already been in stank rotten to the core with animal shit and mold, where he was now was totally different, it was as if this area smelt of decaying animals. Bruce had come across this kind of stench many times during his hiking travels and it was something he was accustomed too and the smell of decaying animals had its own unique smell.

Trying to take in his surroundings he didn't see the wooden poles leaning against the wall when suddenly they went crashing to the ground, hitting what seemed to be used oil drums that had long since been emptied. The echoing noise reverberated through the corridor and if the Bodach was nearby Bruce knew it wouldn't be long before he came looking.

The scenery was stunning with rolling landscapes, streams flowing through the valleys and a mixture of colours ranging from greens to deep oranges flooding the fields and highlands in front of them. It may have been overcast with a slight chill in the air but nevertheless this was a place of natural beauty that hadn't been spoilt by the day to day goings-on of modern life.

Neither of them had spoken much but Pamela was getting more worried about her missing friends and as they walked further out onto the moorlands she kept going over and over the story that Kirsty had told the night before about the Redwood killer and how he still haunts the fields and woodlands surrounding them.

"Kirsty, do you really think that he is still alive? The boy I mean?" she asked.

"Huh? What boy?"

"The Redwood boy, the one whose grave was empty?"

"Oh, that boy. Why? Do you think he still lives in these parts and takes out his revenge on unsuspecting hikers and campers – people like us? I dunno. I bloody hope not." Kirsty replied. "Like Mark said last night, it's just a crazy old story our mams and dads made up to keep us from messing around in the woods. I guess it's just another urban legend."

"Yeah but the murders definitely took place, didn't they? I mean, they were real events that made the news and all that?" Pamela again asked.

"I think so but I can't be sure to be honest with you. I never actually took much interest in that side of it. All I remember is my mam telling me the story I told you guys last night. That's all I know. Why the curiosity – are you scared?"

Pamela felt a chill run down her body as the two girls carried on walking but it was pretty obvious to Kirsty that Pamela didn't know where they were both going.

"Well it is kinda creepy and with the guys missing from camp – well, yeah, it does freak me out a little if I'm being honest."

"Oh, come on Pamela, if he was out there – somewhere – don't you think we would have heard stories on the news, possible sightings and what-not. Stop worrying, I think we are safe enough."

Exhausted from their walk, Pamela stopped for a breather, taking in the view in front of her.

"Anyway, at least it's pretty scenery." said Kirsty in a mocking tone. Then she burst out laughing, a frustrated and tired laugh at that. "So, what's your big plan now? Admit it Pamela, we are lost, aren't we?"

Pamela was tired and didn't want to get into anymore arguments. "We keep going." she replied.

"We keep going? WE KEEP GOING? You know, you're just as dumb as the rest of them Pamela!"

Dark clouds had begun to fill the sky and the brilliant colours of the landscape where now taking on a much duller tone. The cold chill was still there and Pamela didn't want to be caught in the middle of nowhere if and when the weather turned for the worse. More experienced hikers had gotten into serious trouble up on these moors over the years with the local mountain rescue team being called out on numerous occasions and one of the first things Mark mentioned to Pamela before they set off was to keep an eye out on the weather and to be prepared for any eventuality. But this 'eventuality' wasn't something she had planned for and she certainly never thought she would be looking for a mythological house in the middle of nowhere with most of her friends vanishing into thin air!

Taking the lead once again, she decided to carry on going forwards, heading to what looked like small forest in the near distance.

"Hey Kirsty – over there. I think that's where we need to be heading, over there towards that woodland. If the house isn't somewhere around there then we make camp for the night and tomorrow head back to where we came. That's all I can suggest and to be honest, I don't like the look of these clouds. I think its possibly going to get a little wet out here."

Kirsty, having caught up with Pamela took a look towards the sky and then at the forest in the distance in front of her and whilst she didn't like the idea of spending any more time traversing through another one, even she acknowledged that it made sense to get off the open moorland and try and find cover somewhere.

"Yeah, fair enough. I'm not going to be happy though if we don't find this blasted farm." she moaned. "Come with me for a weekend in the woods, he said. It will be fun, he said. Oh, it will be an adventure – HE SAID. Well it certainly is an adventure; I'll say that for Mark!"

The girls headed off down the hillside and towards the forest in the near distance. It would only take them around ten minutes or so to get there just as long as the rain kept away and they kept walking in a brisk fashion.

27

Prowling around in the darkness of the shadows that encapsulated the old ruins, the Bodach could sense every move Bruce was making. He didn't need to go straight for the kill as that would be far too easy. Instead he would take his time, toy with his victim until he loses interest and then he would make his move.

He had a good idea of where he was from the noise of the objects Bruce had knocked onto the floor. The noises reverberated throughout the old building, echoing from room to room giving an indication as to which direction it was coming from. After putting down a jar of his recent collection of body parts removed from Mark's now lifeless body, the Bodach made his way to the door, leaving it open on his way out. He knew every inch of the building, every short cut and every concealed entrance. Making his way from one room to the next, he could hear even the quietest of scuffling noises in the near distance – he was heading directly into Bruce's path.

Having finally made his way towards the end of the corridor, the light that Bruce was hoping would be his savior turned out to be a large split in the corrugated make-shift roof above him that allowed just the briefest of daylight to shine through.

"You got to be kidding me!" he muttered to himself whilst looking up above him with dripping water slowing dripping onto his face.

Looking around he noticed two doors, one directly in front of him with the other just off to his right. Bruce made his way to the first door but having tried hard to push it open it was obvious that something behind it was far too heavy to move out of the way. Giving it a few more heavy pushes with his shoulder he finally gave up trying and decided to make his way to the opposite door.

This time the door was easier to open as there was one single hook keeping it from opening. Slowly lifting the hook up and out of the way the door swung open revealing more jars that were stacked unevenly onto shelves and all where containing items of various shapes and sizes.

Taking one jar from a shelf he hadn't noticed the shadow just off to his left as he proceeded to remove the lid. Struggling to open the jar, Bruce was about to place the axe he had been carrying to the ground just as the Bodach darted back out of the room.

Startled, his grip on the jar loosened, allowing it to crash ontto the floor with all the liquid and bits of flesh mingling with the rest of the grunge that had piled up over the years.

He couldn't be sure if he had seen something or not but Bruce realised he was in a place with no other exits other than the one which he had just come through. Taking a firm grip of the axe, he made his way towards the door.

Fearful of what he may encounter as he passed through room after room, Bruce held onto the axe with both hands – anticipating the worst with each step. Several rooms later he found himself inside what looked like a cattle milking shed with a large round metallic looking vat and several pipelines hanging loosely that were used for extracting milk from the cows.

"Where the fuck am I?" he said to himself.

In front of him was a strange looking container about the size of a chest freezer. It seemed strange that something like this would be here. It just looked out of place. Shaking with fear, Bruce wandered over to it, trying not to make any noise in doing so. Did he really want to see inside? Was he ready for what could be inside? Putting the axe down to one-side he placed both hands onto the door readying himself to open it.

Suddenly, a huge shunting noise came from the direction he had just come from followed by quick shuffling sounds that sounded like someone was making they're towards him. Having already witnessed the strength of the Bodach at first hand, Bruce didn't want to stick around and take a chance of fighting with it. Quickly looking around, he made his way towards the round vat which was located just behind a wall that separated it from the milking pipes and there he squatted down in the darkness, holding in his breath as quietly as he could.

As quickly as he managed to hide, the Bodach appeared at the opposite end of the corridor, pausing and taking in deep breaths whilst listening out for clues as to where Bruce was headed. Looking down towards the floor he lifted his head slowly, his eyes seemingly following the route Bruce had taken. As the figure set off walking past the small looking freezer he stopped in his tracks as he noticed the axe leaning on the wall where Bruce had left it. Turning to pick it up, he knew Bruce was close by but a muffled knocking sound coming from behind him diverted his attention.

Going back to the freezer, he flung open the door to reveal a woman, bound and gagged with blood covering much of her face and body. She was another victim of this masked psycho and she had been forced into this small, confined area that was cold, damp and with a pungent smell of mold. She had been hurt and the pain she was feeling from her abdomen was unbearable. She had no idea how long she had been held captive and she no longer cared. No-one was coming for her and all hope had since long gone.

Looking down on her, the Bodach seemed put-out by this little inconvenience. He had more pressing matters that needed attending too. Raising the axe, he brought it down hard on his hapless victim, slicing into her shoulder causing her to scream out through the gag covering her mouth. The next blow of the axe this time caught the top of her arm just below where he had just hit her but the third and final strike cut deep into the side of her neck, narrowly missing her main artery but still severe enough to cause massive blood loss. His work here was done. Slamming the door down he took a look around before storming off back through the door he originally came from.

Bruce let out a loud gasp, he was safe for now, but for how long he asked himself. And what of the screaming he had heard only moments earlier? Pulling himself up off the floor, he slowly peered around the wall, hoping – just hoping the Bodach had indeed disappeared.

Feeling safe to do so, Bruce made his way to the freezer. From the screaming he had heard he prepared himself for what he was about to see. The door was stiff but after a few seconds of trying he managed to free it open revealing a bloodied woman that had been hacked at by the figure. She had lost a lot of blood and both she and Bruce knew there was very little that could be done to save her. She stared at him but it didn't take long for her eyes to slowly flicker and then close as the last remnants of her life drained away.

Stumbling away from the horror that was in front of him, Bruce, in a state of shock leant back on the wall, squatting down in the darkness, his brain trying to come to terms with the horrors that he had encountered over these last few hours and culminating in watching a woman die in front of him.

Then came the noise of footsteps coming from somewhere in the distance. Loud, stomping footsteps that told him that the Bodach was coming back and this time it would be more serious.

Standing up, Bruce headed towards the end of the corridor and started to run down into an area he hadn't been down before. It was a dead-end!

"Shit!" he said as the sound of the footsteps got increasingly louder.

Turning around to go back to where he came from, he realised it was too late. Stood in the distance and in front of him, the Bodach menacingly mocked him by throwing the axe down onto the ground. He didn't need it. He was far too strong and more powerful than Bruce.

The Bodach proceeded to walk towards Bruce and started to pick up some pace in doing so until he got within a foot or so. Without warning he raised his fist and within an instant he sent Bruce crashing to the ground. Dazed and confused there was very little he could do to protect himself as the Bodach lurched forwards and picked him up. Pinning him to the wall behind him, he was met with a barrage of punches, each finding their intended destination, eventually rendering him unconscious.

28

This time around the woods where far more manageable than the one they had camped in last night with more space and less fodder to trip over, unlike the day before which was a real test of character for inexperienced hikers like Kirsty.

"Why didn't we just camp out here. Look at all the space we have!" she said. "What are we, about an hour away from our camp site?"

"To be fair Kirsty, it was getting dark when we pitched up our tents last night. I don't think anyone would have wanted to carry on walking this far out in the dark, especially not knowing where this place was." Pamela replied.

"Ha! So, you admit we are lost! I knew it."

"No. I didn't say that. I'm merely pointing out that we have walked an hour or possibly less just to get here. I never said we were lost." Pamela said in a light hearted sarcastic tone.

"Alright, so you think the farm is around here somewhere then? Ok, I believe you." replied Kirsty, who was now sitting on the trunk of a fallen tree.

Pamela had walked a little further on towards a clearing in the woods, stopping with her hands on her hips. She raised her head upwards, closing her eyes in the process and muttered something under her breath. Then she turned to Kirsty with a smug like expression on her face.

"Well if we are lost, what is this in front of me?" she replied pointing her left arm to something in the distance but out of view of Kirsty.

Getting up off the tree trunk, Kirsty rubbed the dirt off her backside and the sleeves of her coat before making her way towards Pamela. Then it came into view, a rundown looking building that had most of its windows boarded up with beams of wood that looked like they had been there for years. Parts of the chimneys, two of them, had started to crumble with one of them missing both its chimney pots whereas parts of the roof had started to fall in on itself under the weight of years of decay and the constant lashing of the elements.

The building stood there, like a reminder of its once magnificent past when it was a working farm with its many fields proudly displaying themselves as far as the eye could see. Now they were overgrown and not fit for purpose, taken over by weeds and years of neglect that had long since made them redundant.

There was a barn set further back and just like the main farm it had also fallen into disrepair but with the roof completely gone – collapsing inwardly like that of a freshly baked loaf of bread that had been removed too early from the oven but in this case due to the increment weather and the quick change from hot to cold. Only parts of the outer wall were left standing with the rest of it lying strewn and dotted around on the ground.

"Well, what do you know – the Redwood farm." Pamela triumphantly announced as Kirsty joined up with her.

"And about bloody time too." Kirsty responded. "Come on, let's get in and shelter from these clouds. I don't like the look of them."

"Well what are you waiting for? I'll let you lead the way Kirsty." Pamela gesturing with both her arms in the direction of the farm.

Despite over forty years of neglect and over-grown patches of grass where the garden once was, there still remained a partly covered Yorkshire stone path that led its way up to the main entrance. The door had since long rotted away and had been replaced by a temporary looking blanket of cheap boarding that someone had obviously gone out of their way to erect. It wasn't well fixed and put up little resistance for Pamela as she managed to push open the top half with one easy nudge of her shoulder.

"Here Kirsty, try and kick the bottom half open so we can at least crawl through."

Lodging her foot onto the bottom of the half of the boarded-up doorway, Kirsty managed to force the panel forwards just enough to allow someone of their size to fit through.

Once inside, the true extent of disrepair was clear to see. The walls inside the hallway where tainted with years of black decaying wallpaper that had peeled away in some places and covered in others by green and black mold. A door was being held onto its frame by a single hinge at the bottom and plaster from the ceiling above had partly covered the floor. What was noticeable was how different the temperature was inside compared to the outside as a cold chill permutated throughout the rooms and hallways, seeping in from the crudely placed boards that somebody had taken the time to put up.

"Wow, what a dump!" Kirsty was quick to acknowledge. "And what is the god-awful stench?" as she put her hand towards her nose and mouth.

"You serious Kirsty? How old must this place be and when was the last time somebody actually lived here?" Pamela replied.

"Exactly my point Pamela! Who would want to live here, in the middle of nowhere and miles from your nearest neighbour?"

Making their way past the hallway they felt as if they were alone as there was no sign of anybody, especially hikers, who may have used the building as a make-shift sleepover during their walks. No signs of any previously lit fires, no signs of any empty cans, bottles or wrappings. Nothing to suggest others had been here before.

"JESSICA? MARK? BRUCE?" Pamela shouted out. "ANY OF YOU GUYS HERE?"

"HELLO!" Kirsty joined in. "IF YOU'RE HERE, STOP FUCKING AROUND WILL YOU!"

Kirsty perched herself down on the floor with her back leaning onto a wall.

"Fuck this. I'm taking a rest. They're not here are they?"

Sitting down opposite her, Pamela reached out and rested her hand on Kirsty's knee. "Maybe I got it wrong. Maybe it's not the right house after all and I took the wrong turn or something." she replied.

After a short pause, Kirsty wiped her mouth with the back of her hand as cold sweat had formed over her top lip. "You know, I knew he still liked her. It was obvious. I'm not stupid, I could see the way he was looking at her. I just wish I never came on this stupid camping trip."

This was the first time both girls had actually talked to each other without one of the other trying to pick a fight and Pamela could sympathize with Kirsty.

"You and me both." she replied.

Smiling, Kirsty felt more composed at this point, more than any other time on the trip.

"I swear to god I am never going on another camping trip again." she said.

Breaking out into laughter, both girls finally had some common ground. Both didn't want to be here and both had lost friends that where close to them.

"We're going to have to stay here tonight, aren't we?" Kirsty asked.

Agreeingly, Pamela nodded her head. "Don't see we have any other choice to be honest with you Kirsty."

Checking her pockets, Pamela pulled out her phone, pressing on the buttons whilst holding it in the air. "Right, I'm going to try and find some signal." she said.

"Don't go too far" Kirsty replied with a look of worry on her face.

"Aw, I didn't know you cared."

"I don't! Just don't go too far."

Pamela could understand Kirsty's concerns. She didn't want to be left alone either for too long. It was creepy enough and it didn't help that dark clouds had now filled much of the skyline and with rain now falling adding to the already audible creaking sounds coming from within the building.

As she passed by, Pamela put her hand onto Kirsty's shoulder to give a reassuring sign that everything would be OK. "I'll be back in five minutes. Sit here and just wait for me OK" she said.

Nodding in agreement, Kirsty didn't have any intentions to go wandering alone in this place.

Leaving Kirsty on her own, Pamela took slow turns in and out of the dormant rooms on the ground floor, taking her time to look for any signs of either her friends or other hikers who may have spent some time in this place.

Each room was the same with dust blanketing everything and splintered pieces of old furniture that had been rotting away for years.

Having extinguished all hopes of finding someone she eventually made her way into and through the old kitchen area until she was back outside. The rain had eased considerably but had been replaced by blistering wind and extreme cold.

Outside, Pamela stuttered around the garden area which was now overgrown with weeds, nettles and fallen trees that had accumulated throughout the years, untouched by human hands and the land now seemingly being reclaimed by nature. There was a shed of sorts that had withered from the battering of the elements that had resulted in it collapsing into a heap on the floor and ultimately its final resting place.

Taking out the phone from her pocket, she checked for text messages or possibly a missed call from any of her friends. "Fuck!" Still nothing.

With a sense of defeat, she perched herself down on the remains of the shed, gazing around at the structure of the farm and the uncontrollable mess it was in. For the first time since waking up and noticing her friends missing, reality was finally starting to sink in – something was seriously wrong.

Back inside the building Kirsty had plucked up some courage to go investigating alone, albeit in the rooms Pamela had previously just wandered through. Even though she was scared and didn't plan on wandering around on her own, her mind was starting to play tricks with her so instead of making herself sick with worry it seemed better to look around and keep her herself occupied.

Kicking away bits of old plaster that had fallen from the ceilings she could see that this place had been uninhabited for years with perhaps the Redwood family being the last people to actually live here.

"PAMELA" she shouted out, "Pamela, you in here. Fuck this place is disgusting."

It had been a long day for both girls and the walk had tired them both out but Kirsty was feeling it the most. She had been complaining of feeling lethargic for most parts but the last hour had taken its toll on her. Closing her eyes and placing her hand onto her shoulder, she proceeded to knead the aching muscles that felt tight. Suddenly a loud knocking sound came from the other side of the room. Making her way over she came across a doorway that was blocked with rubble and an old table had been left covering the entrance. She couldn't make out what was in the other room as it was too dark.

Kicking some loose bits of debris away, she managed to drag the table to one-side, just enough to squeeze her body past it and force her way into the darkened room.

It only took a few seconds for her eyes to adjust to the darkness and as she peered into the distance, she could make out what looked like an old stable with ropes dangling down from some rotten beams and rusty metal cattle cages that where just in her line of view. It seemed that the farm had another building attached to it and she was looking directly into it.

"HELLO" she shouted in a shaky voice. "IS ANYBODY DOWN THERE?"

Not getting an answer she started to make her way into the room. "Mark?" she stuttered under her breath. "Mark! I swear to god if that's you I'm gonna make you pay for messing us around like this."

Pausing briefly to try and take in more sounds, she waited several seconds before carrying on walking. Towards the end of the room was a wooden door that seemingly looked out of place. It looked a hell of a lot newer than most of the other parts of the building – like somebody had recently been here and had started to replace parts of it.

This door was fairly easy to open and as she entered the room, she found herself in yet another dank and musty smelling area of the farm. Feeling more and more paranoid that she wasn't alone and just like the first room she had just left, this next one contained evidence that someone had indeed been here before. What looked like fresh hay was piled high in one corner and wooden beams, like the ones used to cover the windows had been neatly stacked together close to a nearby wall. The floor itself looked like someone had attempted to make sure it was free of any obstructing items – unlike all the other rooms she had been in.

Carrying on walking and just like Bruce had done earlier, Kirsty found herself wandering from one room to another until she came across one with yet another of those sliding doors that Jessica, Mark and Bruce had encountered themselves earlier that morning.

Without warning the sound of something heavy and metallic being dragged on the floor came from behind the door in front of her. "Who's there? Hello?" she asked out.

Suddenly the door slid open and crashed onto the frame that was holding it in place and from the darkness he appeared – *THE BODACH*, wearing a chequered red shirt, dirty, muddied and blood-soaked blue denim overalls and that disturbing hessian made mask that hid his eyes.

Storming forwards he swung the sharp-edged axe he was carrying, narrowly missing the now shaken Kirsty who flinched backwards.

The sound of the axe thudding into the wall was enough to make Kirsty snap out of the fear at the sight of the monster that was in front of her. Turning to run back to the other side of the room she had somehow managed to evade him as he readied himself for another swing of the axe.

Not knowing where to go next and knowing he was close-by, Kirsty found herself surrounded by wooden planks as well as the hay that had been piled up against the wall. Without much thought she quickly ran to the hay, squatting down low behind it and covering herself in the smelly, decaying mess just as he appeared from the direction she had just come from. She caught a glimpse of the huge foreboding shadow that had appeared on the wall in front of her as his body blanked out the minimal light within the room.

Dragging the axe on the floor, he sensed she was nearby. He could smell her, taste her almost as he tauntingly took his time to walk a few steps towards where she was hiding.

Behind the hay and with tears now flowing, Kirsty held her hand over her mouth to stifle her breathing and trying not to make any sound as to give away her location. She could just make out the Bodach who was now stood within a few feet of her and it seemed he was also staring right back at her although she couldn't be sure. Closing her eyes and fearing for the worst she stayed there just hoping for him to walk away.

Then with a sudden rush of anger, he lifted and swung his axe at the stacked pile of wooden beams, bringing them crashing down onto the floor. The noise was frightening enough to make Kirsty open her eyes out of fear. The Bodach turned and looked around the room, seemingly expecting to hear something, anything, that would direct him to where Kirsty was hiding and yet he still seemed to be toying with her, like he knew exactly where she was but he would just wait it out until he was fed up of playing this 'hide-and-seek' game.

A few more seconds passed before he turned around and made his way out of the room. Kirsty gasped, taking in as much oxygen as she could. She was safe for now.

29

Pamela looked at the phone again – still nothing, not even the weakest of signals to even try and attempt a call to someone, anyone. "Damn it!" she said.

Standing up, she took another look at her surroundings before heading back towards the farm, taking care not to trip over the overgrown mess that covered large parts of the ground. The remaining parts of the building had weathered badly over the years with thick moss covering the majority of the brickwork. The remaining areas of white exterior paint had either flaked away or dulled in colour over time leaving what once was perhaps an elegant building now looking nothing more than a sad ruin that held a macabre past.

To the side of the main building stood two large out-houses that looked in a much better condition than the others but they were hard to access due to the amount of foliage that had long since overgrown and that had since taken hold of the land and its surroundings.

Pausing for a moment, Pamela thought she heard a noise coming from one of the buildings in front of her. "HELLO?" she shouted out.

Putting the noise down to the surroundings and the wind whistling in and out of the buildings she carried on walking towards to the first out-house. Stopping just in front of the doorway she called out again, more in hope than anything else.

Suddenly a loud cry for help came from inside followed by a terrifying scream that sent a shudder through Pamela's body. "KIRSTY!" she shouted. "KIRSTY – IS THAT YOU?"

Dodging through the thick undergrowth, Pamela managed to find a way into the building but it was too dark and it was impossible to work out where exactly the scream came from.

Taking her time, Pamela started to walk down a long corridor that was mostly blanketed in darkness but for the odd area that was lit by the now fading evening light.

"For crying out loud Kirsty, where the hell are you?"

Kirsty had waited for a few moments before coming out from behind the hay that had concealed her from the Bodach. She knew he would be back so had to make a break for it. Quietly as she could she slowly started to make her way out of the room, keeping her focus solely on the doors around her and trying to hear out for any signs that he may be close-by.

Then without warning a familiar voice came from nearby. "HELLO?" It was Pamela!

Kirsty wanted to shout back but fear and the knowing Bodach could hear her prevented her from doing so.

"Pam… Pamela." she stuttered in a silent tone without hardly moving her mouth. "Pamela, please…" but no sooner had she uttered those few words; a huge crashing sound came from behind her. The Bodach had returned, forcibly pushing away wooden planks and hay from near to the area she had been in hiding. She barely had time to respond by the time he was upon her, his hand gripping around her neck and pinning her to a wall. He was too strong, far too strong for her to do anything and the more she struggled the tighter his grip became until she could barely breath.

Using both her hands, Kirsty tried to push Bodach's hand away from her neck, hitting him relentlessly but to no avail. With breathing becoming more difficult by the second it didn't take too long before she no longer had the energy to fight back.

He could sense the fight in her had gone and using his free hand he reached around his back to release a large hand scythe that he had been carrying. Taunting her in her last moments alive, he lifted the scythe close up to her face, with the tip of the blade just a few centimeters from her eyes. Twisting it, he wanted to make her suffer, to see the panic in her eyes.

She had barely noticed the blade by the time he had retracted it and forced it deep into her abdomen, turning and twisting it in the process. He repeated the process again and again, each time tearing away at her body leaving her entrails protruding from the open wounds.

Throwing the scythe down onto the floor, the Bodach, not content with butchering his powerless victim, proceeded to place his hand inside her open wounds, ripping out various pieces of flesh and dropping it onto the ground, piece after piece. This was pure destruction of a human being with no sense of remorse or feeling.

Pamela had kept quiet for long enough and had walked to the end of the room when suddenly she could hear the thudding of heavy boots coming from in front of her. Stopping to hide in the dark shadows that had concealed pretty much of the room she was in; she peaked her head around the end of a wall to see the Bodach throw something heavy looking down off from his shoulder and onto the ground. In shock, she hid back around the wall, trying to gain her composure before slowly peering her head out of the shadows. She wasn't sure what she had just witnessed but her head was telling her it wasn't good and the noise she was now hearing confirmed to her that whatever it was that he had thrown onto the ground, it was definitely something heavy!

The Bodach was raining down blow after blow down onto the ground but she still couldn't see what he had hitting. Trying as hard as she could to get a better view, there was some heavy looking machinery in her way. Again, he raised his arms and she managed to glance at what he was holding - an axe, before he brought it down one more time.

Fixated on the sight in front of her she watched as the Bodach kneeled down and started to tug on something on the ground when after a few seconds of struggling he raised himself up back onto his feet, revealing what he had been hacking away it.

Recoiling in horror, Pamela instantly knew what it was – it was part of a human leg and from the colour of the pants, although drenched in blood and along with the shoe that was still attached, she soon realized that this belonged to Kirsty and the Bodach had been hacking away at her lifeless body all that time.

With her back to the wall all kinds of emotions swept through her. *"Surely this couldn't be the Redwood killer, The Bodach that Mark and Kirsty had spoken about last night? No, this was just too far-fetched. This couldn't be really happening!"*

A few moments passed and she decided to glance one more time at the monster that was still using his axe as some sort of butchering device and with the sound of the blade striking down with such force and the noise of bones breaking, this was enough to convince Pamela that she needed to get away - as far away as she could.

Trying to keep calm she slowly turned away from the grisly sight behind her and made her way towards the end of the corridor, making sure not to catch anything that could make any noise. The doorway was only a few feet away and although it was now a little darker outside, she felt it would be better to take her chances out in the woods rather than be anywhere near the farm building's.

Rushing to the door, she managed to escape out into the yard and into the overgrown lawn, stumbling on hidden bracken and other discarded rubble.

With tears streaming down her face and full of emotion, she hadn't seen the strange figure lurking inside the kitchen as she drew closer to the steps leading up to the door.

Upon entering and out of breath, Pamela stopped and took a second to look behind her to make sure she hadn't been followed.

"Don't make a fucking sound." suddenly came a man's voice.

Instinctively she started to turn her head but was stopped as the voice got more and more threatening. "Don't look at me! Don't fucking look at me!"

Keeping her eyes focused on the outside she felt him shuffle up close behind her. "Keep your eyes front and your fucking mouth shut." he said. "Now when I say move, we move. You understand? You don't look behind you, you hear me. Don't. Look. Back."

Grabbing hold of Pamela's arm, he forcefully dragged her away from the door. "Now move." he instructed.

30

Walking back in towards the main room of the farm, Pamela noticed several crudely made crosses that had been hammered onto the walls leading from the hallway she and Kirsty had originally entered from. She hadn't noticed them before but compared to the rest of the house these looked relatively clean, as if made by someone perhaps in the last couple of years or so. As crude as they where they seemed to fit in with the look of the building in its decrepit state.

"Stop!" came the strangers voice. "Don't go any further."

Pamela, still not sure as to what his intentions were turned around to face him. "Look, I don't know who you are, where you are from or how you got here but there is something seriously fucked up with this place and I don't want to stay around here much longer!" she said in a rushed tone. "I think I've just seen one of my friends butchered back there by a mad-man and I think he may also have taken more of my friends."

Around them, cold air was whipping in and out of the rooms through the many cracks and crevices that had appeared over time and yet this didn't seem to faze him. Instead he stood there with a menacing look, pointing his rifle directly at Pamela.

"You people. You think this is a fucking game. You have no idea what this thing can do. It has no end. This - this is just the beginning." he said.

"What are you talking ab - " Pamela was about to speak but he cut her off instantly. "Shut the fuck up!" he snapped back.

"Right now, he's out there watching, waiting."

Lowering his rifle, he proceeded to take a couple of steps towards Pamela, always with his eyes firmly on her.

"Like many other people I never believed in the stories or the folklore surrounding this place. Yes, the murders took place but all this bullshit about the farmer's son returning from the grave to seek revenge on all those that come close to finding this house – well I never fucking believed in any of it – until my daughter, who was just like you – young, innocent – she never returned home that night." he said.

"Amy, that was her name. She was nineteen years old and I've waited ten years, TEN long years and I've been coming up here, searching for something, just – anything, ever since."

Finally, his gaze fell away from Pamela as he began to look around the room they were standing in, turning away from her and taking steps towards an old looking fireplace that was littered in loose papers and other remnants of the past.

"How long have you been following us, me and Kirsty I mean?" Pamela asked. "Have you been here all the time? Did you see my friend being taken by that bastard thing back there?"

"Have you been using us as, as bait!" she demanded to know.

Turning around, the stranger looked more pissed off than he did earlier. "You listen and listen good. You get out of here - now while you can. You run and you keep running and you don't EVER come back. Don't ever look back. Whatever this thing is it killed my daughter and now it wants to kill you."

"But my friends, they might be here." Pamela replied.

"Have you listened to a fucking word I've said. Your friends are dead!" the stranger replied with a chilling smirk on his face. "Oh yes, the legend is most definitely true. Wouldn't you agree?"

"So, you have been watching us! You bastard! You could have stopped them, all of us from coming up here and you didn't! You could have warned us." Pamela screamed back at him.

"And would you have believed me if I did try to stop you? I would have been a fucking weirdo telling nothing but a camp fire story and nothing more! Don't make me laugh." he replied.

"But no, I never saw your friends being brought here and I've not seen any of them until now, until I saw you and that other girl wandering around out in the woods nearby. I followed you both here but that's it. I've not seen any of your other friends but let's be sure of one thing – they are dead, absolutely fucking dead!"

Whether or not it was out of sheer stupidity or plain ignorance, Pamela was defiant. "Well I'm not leaving with them!" she said.

The stranger shook his head before looking up at Pamela who was by now scurrying around seemingly looking for something.

"What are you doing?" the stranger asked.

"I'm looking for something to defend myself with. If you're not going to help me then I'll have to do it on my own." she replied.

"You got to be kidding me." The stranger could see she was being serious. "Fucks sake! What part of get out of here didn't you understand?" he said. "OK, if we do this, we do it my way! You do exactly as I say, when I say. Got it?"

Sensing the stranger's reluctance to help her she walked over to him, pausing a couple of feet away and with a nodding motion she muttered in agreement. "Fine!" she said.

31

"Over the years I've been coming to this place, checked inside-out but somethings changed. I don't know why this thing has come back but it's using it as some kind of fucking mortuary." the stranger said whilst forcing open one of the many doors that had been closed within the corridor where Pamela witnessed Kirsty being slaughtered. "And in all those years I've never come this close to confronting it."

Pamela was staring towards the cold looking machinery where Kirsty's body was cut into pieces by the Bodach. She wanted to walk over, to see with her own eyes what that bastard had done but an overwhelming sense of shock came over her.

"Don't even go there" the stranger warned her. He could sense her intentions and whilst he never saw Kirsty being murdered, he just knew what lay in that corner.

Pamela, her eyes still gazing towards that area didn't respond.

"Hey, you hear me? HEY, SNAP OUT OF IT!"

Hearing the strangers raised voice for the second time, Pamela shook her head and turned to face the stranger. "Yeah, I heard you. Let's go." she replied.

Pushing some loose debris away that covered the entrance to the door, Pamela made her way through and into another darkened room. The stranger followed close behind her, still clutching his rifle and readying himself for what could possibly lay ahead of them.

Suddenly and without any warning, a huge silhouette appeared behind them. Neither of them saw it and neither of them heard anything. The Bodach was following them!

Inside the room and just like all the others Pamela had been in, it was in sorry state with more paint peeling away from the walls and any remaining furniture that had been discarded over the years was now covered in moss and mold. Everything felt damp, the walls, the furniture – even the air had a damp feel and smell to it.

Pamela made her way into the center of the room, trying her best not to touch anything, all the time her eyes were struggling to adjust to the darkness.

"Over there, we can go that way." she said pointing towards an open walkway.

"Wait, what was that?" the stranger said, turning around quickly to see what was behind him.

"What, I didn't hear anything?"

"I thought I heard something. Something behind me."

Slowly he raised his rifle, aiming it towards the darkness within the doorway and with his thumb he pulled back the hammer on his rifle.

"I suggest you leave, now!" he whispered to Pamela.

"What? I don't understand."

"Get the fuck out of here, NOW!" he shouted just as the Bodach appeared within the doorway, its huge mass filling the void with its mask piercing through the darkness. It stood there, watching the stranger, heavy breathing with its chest puffed out and its head flinching from left-to-right. *It was readying itself!*

Pamela instantly took off, running into yet another adjoining corridor. She could hear the sound of the stranger's rifle being shot but didn't stop to see what was happening, instead she kept running until she came to a closed door. Sliding it open, she stumbled into another room and waited for the stranger to catch up.

It was only seconds but to Pamela it felt longer as she could hear the strangers rifle again being used. Then just as quick as she heard it being fired the stranger appeared in front of her, instantly turning around to close the door behind him. Struggling to keep it closed, the Bodach was pulling on the handle from the opposite side, the stranger yelled to Pamela to take his rifle.

"I CAN'T!" she shouted back.

"ARRGHHH, TAKE IT, TAKE THE DAMNED GUN!" he screamed back, struggling to keep the door closed.

Now crying and fearful she repeated herself. "I can't."

"TAKE THE FUCKING RIFLE!" he yelled back whilst holding out his arm.

She could see the stranger couldn't hold the door for much longer, the Bodach was far stronger than he was. Running over to him, she snatched hold of the rifle just as his grip on the door was loosening.

"NO GO. GO!" he shouted. "You've got one round left, one round. Make it count." as his grip on the door slipped and he fell onto the ground.

Knowing there was little she could now do to help the stranger; she turned and ran towards the opposite side of the room and exited out through another door.

32

The Bodach stood there, an overwhelming bulkiness that not even the strongest of men could possibly defend themselves against and yet it didn't rush in, it didn't need too. It could see the stranger was now defenseless, unarmed and with nowhere to go. It could take his time.

Instead it turned to face a wall that had all sorts of farming tools hanging down, all rusty with age. After a moment pause it lifted one off and away from the hook that was holding it in place, it was a scythe.

The stranger slowly got to his feet and walked, seemingly casually towards the exit in which Pamela had just left through. But he didn't follow her, he didn't want too. He wanted to say and fight the monster. He wanted it to pay for murdering his daughter.

"Makes no different to me. Whether I live or whether I die."

The stranger could hear the footsteps of the Bodach walking up behind him but he wasn't scared. He had lost all sense of fear the moment he passed his rifle over to Pamela.

Turning to face his nemesis he knew this was only going to end in one way. "Death comes to us all, it's just a matter of how and when. You killed my daughter - I died a long time ago." he said.

"Day after day I've waited for this moment. So why don't you look me in the fucking eye you cowardly bastard! Why don't you show me what you've really got?"

Holding out his arms, the stranger started to antagonize the Bodach. "Do it! FUCKING DO IT!" he shouted.

The Bodach just stood there, listening to everything the stranger was saying but its grip on the scythe was tightening. The stranger proceeded to walk forwards, still antagonizing it.

"Do it. DO IT!"

Suddenly the stranger felt a stinging pain shoot through his abdomen and within a few seconds blood coursed up through his throat and into his mouth.

Falling to his knees and placing his hand to his stomach, he felt the warm flow of blood oozing from the wound inflicted by the

Bodach. Spitting out blood that was filling his mouth he looked up to see the Bodach standing dominantly over him.

"Fucking do it." He could barely speak by now as the Bodach raised the scythe above his head and brought it down, severing deep into the stranger's neck.

33

Through the maze of corridors that ran throughout the farm and its buildings, the echoing sounds of the stranger's screams as he lay dying reverberated all around. The chilling last shrill he made stopped Pamela in her tracks as she gripped tightly onto the rifle he had given her for protection.

In tears and with no idea where she was going, she stood there, cupping her mouth to stop her from crying out loudly. The Bodach had taken her friends, butchered Kirsty in front of her eyes and now seemingly done the same with the stranger – it was only a matter of time before he came after her. Reality was setting in that all the corridors, rooms and hallways she had been in would never let go of her. They had tangled her up like a spider's web does to a fly and she was the prey that the Bodach was now hunting.

The screaming of the final death throes coming from the stranger had dissipated into the cold air by the time she plucked up the courage to go further into the darkness but with the Bodach not too far behind it was now all or nothing.

Walking further into the corridor a smell she had noticed in all the other rooms had started to get stronger with each step. It was a distinctive and yet a sickly-sweet odour that she had smelt earlier on as soon as her and Kirsty went into the main farm building but this time it was far much worse.

With her hand over her nose and mouth she turned left into another corridor, taking her time to do so as the smell was now making her wretch. No matter what, she knew she had to go this way if she didn't want to face the Bodach again.

That's when she caught sight of them - bodies, lots of them, all hung up by their wrists with a rope of sorts wrapped around a metal bar above them.

She didn't have time to think about what to do so reluctantly she made her way past the first body, pushing him slowly out of the way. It was a man, around his mid-thirties and casually dressed in walking gear, possibly a family man whose wife and children are out looking for him right now but she couldn't think about that, she knew she had to keep going.

Two, three, four – the bodies kept mounting up but then, unexpectedly one of them, a woman, opened her eyes slightly as Pamela tried to move her out of the way. She was covered in blood and, like all of his other victims, had a gag wrapped around her mouth. Trying to get Pamela's attention, she tried to say something but Pamela fought off any urges to help her. *"I'm sorry, I'm sorry."* she muttered as she tried pushing her to one side. The woman was getting louder, screaming almost, through the bloody gag in her mouth. Not wanting the Bodach to hear, Pamela quickly put her hand over the woman's mouth to muffle out the sound. *"Please, please, I'm sorry."* she kept repeating.

The woman stopped and her eyes focused on something moving behind Pamela. Quickly and almost instinctively, Pamela looked around and saw all the bodies swaying in unison – the Bodach was coming!

Forcing her way past the remaining bodies, Pamela headed through and out of the corridor and found herself inside a stable of sorts with hay covering much of the floor and a doorway that was blocked with corrugated metal.

She could hear the footsteps of the Bodach as he made his way past the hanging bodies and in a panic, she tried to cock the rifle so it was ready to use. Struggling, she didn't have time as the Bodach made his way around and into the stable and never once braking his stride, he made his way to Pamela, grabbing the rifle out of her grasp and punching her in the face all in an instant.

Grabbing her by the back of her neck, he picked her up and then threw her towards a bale of hay with such force it almost winded her. Dazed and bloodied, Pamela didn't have time to defend herself as the Bodach was upon her yet again, grabbing her by her throat and raining down punch after punch onto her face. It was endless, merciless - as he stood over her, not taking any breaks in between the incessant beating.

She didn't know what happened next but as she found herself on the floor and with hardly any energy left, she noticed through her puffed up and bloodied eyes the figures of two people fighting. Struggling to make the images clearer she soon started to realise that the Bodach was being held back by another man – it was Bruce!

"Go!" he shouted to Pamela.

He was holding his side and in obvious pain but he still had enough strength to keep the Bodach away from Pamela.

"Pamela, go!" he continued just as the Bodach grabbed him by the neck and with brute strength he punched his hand directly into Bruce's abdomen, ripping out pieces of flesh before tossing him to the ground.

Picking herself up, she saw the stranger's rifle on the ground next to her. This was her chance – *"one bullet, make it count"* – the stranger told her!

The Bodach started to make his way towards Pamela and just as she grabbed hold of the rifle, she managed to find the time to turn around, aiming it directly at him.

"FUCK YOU!" she shouted as she pulled the trigger.

The Bodach took a step back as the bullet ripped into his chest and out from the other side. Falling onto his knees, the monster put one hand over the wound, looking down at the blood that was now covering his hand, before falling over onto his back.

Sitting on the ground, Pamela looked on in shock at seeing the body of the monster that had slain her friends. *Had she really killed him?* She couldn't be sure.

It took several minutes before she had the energy to pick herself up off the floor, walking over to the Bodach she kicked his legs to see if there was any movement. Nothing happened.

Slowly, she made her way over the Bruce, kneeling down beside him and it was then she realised that he had given his life to save hers. Rubbing away the tears that were streaming down her eyes and cheeks, she muttered a thank you but knowing there was nothing more she could do for him she still had to get out of the building and try and find help.

Leaving Bruce behind Pamela limped away and out of the room, still crying from all that she had seen and witnessed. She passed from one room to another, dragging her broken body along despite all the pain she was in – and then she saw her, Jessica, her lifeless body lying on a table with her abdomen completely ripped open and intestines strewn over her chest.

Tears started to form in Pamela's eyes as she started upon her best friend. "Jes---sica." she spoke in a soft, quite tone.

34

Room after room, there were all the same as Pamela wandered through the farm buildings. She was in plenty of pain by the time she stumbled into one that seemed out of place in comparison to the grimy, derelict ones she had already encountered. This one had fresh hay, clean looking water in a trough and even the smell wasn't as pungent as some of the others. It was like this part of the farm was being cared for.

In one corner she noticed a set of ladders that seemed to go directly up to the roof but it was too dark for her to see properly. As this was perhaps her last hope of escape Pamela had no other option but to climb them and hope for the best!

The ladders went all the way up to a hatch of sorts but years and years of neglect had allowed all kinds of debris to cover it, making it difficult to open. Pamela pushed as hard as she could to open it but nothing happened, not even the slightest of movement until suddenly and with a burst of energy flowing through her tired and broken body, she managed to prise it open – only an inch or so but it was a start!

Whether or not it was pure adrenaline or something else that gave her the strength, she managed to fling open the hatch after a few more minutes of struggling. Dragging herself up and out into the night air and taking in a deep gasp – she was free.

Emotionally, Pamela didn't know whether to laugh or cry as she stood there, taking in the view of the old farm house and its surrounding buildings. Bloodied and cold she afforded herself a quick grin, acknowledging the fact she was still alive but that was short lived as reality set in that all of her friends were still in there, butchered by a madman.

Snapping out of the daze she was in, she started to walk through the dense undergrowth, still holding her side as pain traversed through her upper body. Still bloodied from the pounding the Bodach had given out to her she made her way out from the evil clutches of the farm and into the fields that had been lit up by the bright moon light that shone like a torch paving her way out to safety.

The further away from the farm she got the more energy she was finding until she managed to form some sort of fast pace that seemed to spur her on further until having looked back over her shoulder, the silhouette of the farm finally disappeared into the blackness of the night.

Pamela kept on going, not wanting to stop for even a second just in case the Bodach was still alive – possibly hunting her. She passed through fields and struggled through hedgerows until finally she found a road, one that looked like it was used regularly.

Collapsing onto her knees and out of breath she knew she couldn't go any further. This is where it ends, she thought to herself as she finally succumbed to the pain and tiredness that she had valiantly fought off for so long. Lying herself down on the road, she could do nothing more than hope that she would be found, alive.

The Bodach lay there, bleeding profusely from the gunshot wound inflicted upon him by Pamela. Knocked unconscious from the impact the bullet made as it ripped into him from close range, he could do nothing to stop her from escaping nor could he do anything to prevent her from finding help.

Waking from his slumber he managed to pull himself up off the ground, struggling to keep his balance as he put one hand on the wall. Taking a few moments for his brain to process the pain he was in and to plan his next move he slowly made his way out of the stable and headed towards another room that had huge amounts of wooden pallets and bales of hay all congregated together in one corner and opposite was an iron table that consisted of various tools and equipment used for repairing machinery.

Tearing a handful of hay away from its bale he headed to the iron table, placing the hay down next to several rolls of old looking tape. Looking down towards his chest he saw fresh blood still oozing out from the bullet wound and onto his filth ridden chequered shirt.

After tearing away a small section of his shirt, the Bodach picked up the hay and forced it into the hole on his chest. The pain intensified as the sharp jagged edges scratched deep into his body. Picking up the tape from the table, he tore off strips and covered the now blood-soaked hay before crudely patching up his shirt with the remaining strips.

Knowing his victim was still at large and knowing people would come looking, the Bodach slowly made his way through the corridors and out of the farm into the still darkness of the night.

He wasn't going to stop until he found her.

35

The bright lights that seemed to shine from the distance felt like the warm hands of safety as she struggled to keep her eyes open. The damp, cold air of the night was starting to take its toll on her body as she lay on the road shivering and in pain but the noise coming from the distance gave her some much needed reassurances she was going to make it.

Finding the energy to pull herself onto her knees, Pamela waved one arm in the air as the white van came around the corner in front of her. The driver didn't see her until a deep bump in the road caused his van to lurched upwards and the headlights shone directly onto her. Within an instant, he pressed down hard on the breaks bringing the vehicle to a stand-still just feet away from her.

"WHAT THE FUCK!" he shouted, seeing the bloodied face of Pamela directly in front of him.

Getting out of the van, hesitant at first, he stood behind the open door, not really knowing what to do.

"You, you OK?" he asked.

Not getting a response he slowly closed the van door and walked towards Pamela who was stood frozen in the bright headlights.

"Hey, are you OK?" he asked again. "What the hell has happened?"

Looking up, Pamela reached out and put her arms around him, wanting to feel the safety of another person.

"Listen, let's get you out of here alright. It looks like we need to get you to a hospital." he said.

Pamela still hadn't spoken. She couldn't find the words to even try and explain what had happened these last few hours nor did she think he would ever believe her despite the condition she was in.

Releasing himself from her hold, the man slowly ushered her towards his van. "Come on, let's get you out of here."

She didn't know how long she had been sleeping as she passed out pretty quickly as soon as the man had started to drive away. It was still dark however and it looked to have been raining at some point as the trees surrounding the now parked up van looked shiny in the moonlight.

The driver gently tapped Pamela on the shoulder, just hard enough to jolt her from her sleep. In a panic, she sat upright in the seat, scared at the sight of the stranger sat opposite her.

"Hey, it's me. It's just me" he said. "I don't want to scare you, but I think I've taken a wrong turn."

"Wha – what do you mean you've taken a wr - wrong turn?" stuttered Pamela.

"For all I know we've been going around in circles. All the roads look the same out here."

"Well, where are we?"

"I don't know"

Looking out of the window, Pamela flinched at the sights around her. Everything looked far too familiar.

"WAIT, WHERE ARE YOU GOING?" she shouted as the man started to leave the van.

"We just passed a house back there. I'll go and get some help" he responded. "You're safe!"

Closing the door, the stranger started to walk off towards a building in the distance. Not feeling safe, Pamela began fearing that all this felt too familiar. Alone in the woods with no clue as to where she was – something didn't feel right.

Getting out of the van, she shouted to the stranger who was only a few metres away.

"HEY!"

"What's wrong" he replied.

"What did you mean we've been driving around in circles?"

"Don't worry about that. Look, the house is two minutes away. I'll be right back."

Pamela sensed something was wrong, everything about this was definitely wrong! The way the stranger was dressed, similar to that of the Bodach with his tartan shirt and blue overalls and the way he spoke was far too casual considering he had found her slumped on the road, covered in blood and getting no explanation from her. *It all felt wrong.*

With her eyes looking downwards and a puzzled expression on her face, realisation set in. "But there is no other house around here" she replied.

The stranger had carried on walking towards the house but didn't say anything back. *"He must have heard me."* she thought to herself.

Split between staying at the van or following the stranger in the hope her fears were nothing more than delusional, Pamela decided to follow him.

The road they followed eventually led to a yard that contained dozens of scrapped vehicles. Cars, vans and motorcycles scattered the area and the smell of oil and petrol filled the air. *"Why hadn't we noticed this place before?"* she thought.

And then it appeared through a break in the line of cars that had been stacked on top of each other – the farm and its out-houses that she so desperately managed to escape only a short time ago! They had entered it from a different location to the one she and Kirsty originally had.

"WHAT THE FUCK!" she screamed just as the stranger stopped and turned to face her.

"Don't be afraid." he said. "He won't hurt you now I'm here."

"You, you – you know this place? You brought me back here? Who are you?" Pamela stuttered.

"I figured you must have found your way up here, being covered in blood and all. The scared expression on your face when I met you on the road. He's been sloppy this time. No-one has ever left this place; he simply won't allow it – I won't allow it!"

"I don't understand?"

"Understand? What is there to understand?" the man gazed back at Pamela with a crazed smile on his face.

"You lot are all the fucking same. You come up here, to see for yourselves the home of the famous Redwood killer, believing or not in the stories your parents used to tell you. And when you do find this place you piss your pants when he appears."

"What did you expect to happen? Did you think he would take photographs with you and sign autographs!"

"YOU'RE INSANE!" screamed back Pamela. "I don't know why you protect him or what you are to him but you are fucking insane!"

Taking a few steps backwards she hadn't noticed the dark mass appearing slightly behind the stranger when out of nowhere and with one quick glance of his axe, he brought it down hard onto the stranger's head, killing him instantly as he fell to the ground.

Seeing the slaughter taking place in front of her, Pamela started to run back towards the van. It wasn't the wisest of choices but it was her only place to go as these woods belonged to the Bodach and no amount of running would be enough to evade him.

Making her way back, she managed to get into the passenger side of the van, locking it behind her. Sitting there in fear and not being able to see where the Bodach was there was very little she could do when suddenly and out of the darkness the window next to her was shattered as the Bodach swung his axe into the glass. Reaching his arm inside, he managed to release the lock before forcing open the door.

Scrambling across to the driver's seat, Pamela did not have enough time to free herself as the Bodach grabbed hold of her foot, dragging her back to his side. Kicking and screaming she managed to land a few blows onto his covered face, enough to make him lose his grip on her.

Forcing herself out of the van, Pamela managed to get herself onto her feet and headed off into the woods before the Bodach could reach her. Her only hope now was to go back to where all this began and just hope she can find a way to end it all once and for all.

She was in severe pain as she ran towards the farm, holding her left side and trying hard not to slow down. Every step was as painful as the last but she could hear him not too far behind, his heavy bulk crunching the fallen branches and leaves on the ground. She glanced back, only for a second and noticed he was limping badly – possibly injured from the gunshot wound she had inflicted on him earlier.

Making her way through the forest, she headed back towards yard containing the scrapped vehicles. Perhaps if she could hide in one of cars, he may lose track her, she thought to herself.

Back in the yard, she went from car to car but all the doors were locked and with all the windows closed, she was now struggling to hide.

"DAMN IN!" she screamed out, whilst running to the next car.

Exhausted and with hope fading, she could hear the Bodach slowly making his way into the yard, his heavy footsteps dragging on the gravel. He was struggling but what good was that if she couldn't defend herself.

Realising she had nowhere to hide she started to look around for something, anything to help protect herself with. With very little laying around and with no time to keep looking she picked up a metal rod that was rooted into the ground, leaning next to one of the cars.

The pole was heavy but manageable as she tried to quietly make her way towards a small yellow car that had been placed directly under a mechanical grabber.

Meanwhile, the Bodach was making his way towards the mangled cars, keeping his footsteps to a minimum in the hope of hearing for any sign as to where Pamela was hiding.

Passing the yellow car Pamela was hiding behind, he never noticed her crawling around the opposite side.

"HEY!" she shouted as she struggled onto her feet.

The Bodach quickly turned, only to be met with the heavy blow of the metal rod striking him to the side of his head. Before he had time to react, another blow, this time to the other side of his head knocked him to the ground.

With pain shooting through her body and with hardly any strength left, Pamela found the energy to carry on raining down heavy blows onto the Bodach. He was struggling and she could sense it!

Crowding over him, she lifted the rod with its point facing downwards but before she could end this once and for all the Bodach reached out, grabbing hold of her right leg and with one firm tug, he managed to knock her to the ground, making her drop the rod in the process. Putting her hand out to break her fall, she landed on the side of her broken ribs. Pain instantly taking her breath away.

The Bodach managed to get onto his feet but although the beating had left him dazed he still found a way to get to Pamela before she could get up.

Kneeling down, he grabbed her by the neck and with a firm grip he slowly started to squeeze the life from her. Struggling to breathe, she tried to knock his hand away but he was too strong.

The Bodach was only a few seconds away from claiming his final victim when all of a sudden, his grip was released from around her neck. A numbing pain shot through his body as he let out a loud scream and slumping away from her, he saw the metal rod sticking out from the side of his rib cage.

Scrambling with her hands, Pamela had managed to find the rod and with barely enough strength to muster she had impaled the Bodach.

It may have only been a few seconds but it seemed like an eternity as Pamela rose to her feet. Yanking the rod out of the Bodachs side, she stood over him, looking down with no pity or remorse. He had taken everything away from her, now it was her turn to take everything away from him. *Everything!*

Lifting the rod high above her head she let out a loud scream before bringing it down, swinging it onto his skull with such force the noise of it cracking reverberated off the metal, rusting vehicles around them.

He was beaten. His body lying there at the mercy of his final victim. But just to be sure, Pamela raised the rod for one last time and with the point again facing downwards she made no mistake as it found its way into his skull and rooting itself firmly into the ground below him.

The Bodach flinched for a few seconds, his arm flailing in the air, attempting to grab hold of the rod Pamela still had hold of. She watched on, making sure it was out of his reach and as his arms slowly fell to the ground, she pulled the rod into a sideward position, splitting his skull in the process.

Letting go, Pamela stumbled backwards a couple of feet until her legs buckled beneath her. The adrenaline that had served her so well in those last few minutes had deserted her and with no energy left she could nothing more than collapse onto the ground.

The lifeless body of the Bodach lay there in front of her as she lifted her head towards the dark sky. Shaking with emotion she paused for a few seconds before looking back towards the Bodach.

"Fucking farmers!" she nervously said to herself.

THE END

Printed in Great Britain
by Amazon